About the Author

Rachel Flouskos is a queer Australian writer. She lives with her wife and three pets. When she is not writing, she is painting, reading or walking along the beach in the tiny beach-side town that she lives in.

The Princess of Whystelkine

R Flouskos

The Princess of Whystelkine

Olympia Publishers
London

www.olympiapublishers.com
OLYMPIA PAPERBACK EDITION

Copyright © R Flouskos 2024

The right of R Flouskos to be identified as author of
this work has been asserted in accordance with sections 77 and 78 of
the Copyright, Designs and Patents Act 1988.

All Rights Reserved

No reproduction, copy or transmission of this publication
may be made without written permission.
No paragraph of this publication may be reproduced,
copied or transmitted save with the written permission of the publisher,
or in accordance with the provisions
of the Copyright Act 1956 (as amended).

Any person who commits any unauthorized act in relation to
this publication may be liable to criminal
prosecution and civil claims for damage.

A CIP catalogue record for this title is
available from the British Library.

ISBN: 978-1-80439-868-5

This is a work of fiction.
Names, characters, places, and incidents originate from the writer's
imagination. Any resemblance to actual persons, living or dead, is
purely coincidental.

First Published in 2024

Olympia Publishers
Tallis House
2 Tallis Street
London
EC4Y 0AB

Printed in Great Britain

Dedication

For those who don't know where they belong.

Acknowledgements

I came up with the idea for this book while I was on my honeymoon. This book lived in the Notes app on my phone for months. Between work and other things, I would jot down some ideas in the app, never truly believing that a publication would be within reach.

I couldn't have written a book without the support of my wife, Jay-Dean, who believed in me when I didn't. She helped me through some truly devastating times, and she was my champion through this whole process. She stayed up for hours with me, dedicating as much of her time as I did mine to the plot and development of this book. She's suffered through every possible version of this story; the good edits and the bad ones. She has been my truest compass, and my truest friend.

I'd also like to thank my brother, Bobby, who gave me more than his fair share of reviews and suggestions. His blunt honesty helped me decide where I wanted this story to go, and who I was truly writing it for.

To everyone who has ever felt lost, or like they don't belong, I hope you find your place in this book and with these characters.

I hope you find yourself here, in this story.

Prologue

In a small kingdom by the sea, the air is cool, and the night is silent. Nothing can be heard in the night but heavy waves crashing violently on the rocky beach and the howl of the salty wind over the ocean. The brisk air blows in eerie silence as the little, tired kingdom sleeps in undisturbed slumber.

The uneven red sand on the ground of the kingdom reflects a glow from the moon above. Buildings throughout the kingdom are made of exposed grey stone, rough from salt erosion and strong winds. Leaves from nearby trees rustle and sing the song of a windy seaside. Dim streetlamps create little puddles of yellow light over the dusty roads, trickling through the town and attracting insects.

Under the starry night, in the light of a full moon, a dark-hooded figure climbs the stone wall of a castle. The wind is cold, blowing the hood back to reveal a young woman's face, surrounded by thick, black curls.

A baby cries.

In a small room of a high tower, a cradle rocks in the wind. A baby, no more than a month old, with a single golden curl and pointed ears bellows into the dead of the night.

Gentle fingers stroke the baby's cheek. Tender, longing eyes—a look that could only belong to someone who longed for a baby of their own—look down at the child. The baby's fist grasps a long finger, with a grip so tight it cuts the circulation to the fingertip. A desperate longing aches inside the hooded figure.

Under the cover of darkness, the hooded figure snatches the baby from the cradle in the high tower of a castle.

A horse gallops. Horses' hooves kick dust into the air, rising in brown smoke around the castle tower. In a cloud of red dust, the horse is gone.

The quietness of the nursery alerts the parents. Terror-stricken is the face of a young mother when she finds an empty cradle. Nothing in the cradle but a single strand of curly black hair. Piercing green eyes desperately look for a sign. A blood-curdling scream awakens a bearded father, who commands a kingdom-wide search for a green-eyed and golden-haired elven baby.

Until the sun rises in the east, the kingdom searches.

No sign is found.

Chapter 1

26 Years Later

It's an exciting day. The sunlight peeking in through my bedroom window warms my face, turning my cheeks the slightest tinge of rosy pink. I am lounging on my window seat, in my palace in Willcrest, our tired seaside kingdom in Nashwalte, leaning over the windowsill. The scent of purple peonies fills my nostrils as I look out at the forests beyond the castle, my mind blissfully vacant.

Behind me, my lady-in-waiting, Hazel, whistles cheerily as she picks dresses made of tulle and delicate fabrics from the wardrobe and places them neatly in a floral-printed suitcase, embroidered with my initials: AN. Hazel flattens each garment as she places it, smoothing it down to make more room for yet more clothing. Her whistle calms me. It reminds me of a lullaby sung in my native tongue that my late mother would sing when I was young.

"Should you need a coat for your travels, or shall I pack it, Your Highness?" Hazel offers politely.

Although I am looking out the window at the green pastures and mountains outside the kingdom walls, daydreaming, I wave her off, expecting that she will do what she pleases anyway. Hazel is the best lady-in-waiting in the kingdom – I should know, I've had many over the years. But she can be very stubborn. Perhaps that is why I have not fired her. Yet.

"How should I know?" is all I say in reply. "You have done more travelling than I have. What do you think?"

"Well, I don't know," Hazel answers thoughtfully, smoothing the velvet coat down with the palm of her hand. "I've only travelled as far as the Berjora Islands. Where you're going is much farther, Your Highness."

A birdsong chorus from the green woods on the outskirts of the kingdom distracts me. It brings my attention back to the pine trees and green meadows. I had always imagined myself disappearing into the woods and living among the birds and woodland animals. I often daydream of sleeping in the arm of a tree, using the leaves and dens as shelter, feasting on whatever berries and nuts I could forage from the surrounding areas. It's a nice thing to think about, abandoning my royal duties and running away to the forest, but I would never really do it.

"Your Highness!" Hazel's frustrated voice cuts through my imagination.

When I turn back to look at her, my long dark braids flicking around my shoulder as I do so, I notice that Hazel is now showing me several pairs of shoes, a firm expression on her face. There's a deep line between her thick eyebrows, her eyes drilling into mine.

Hazel has quite a pretty face for a lady-in-waiting. She has caramel eyes and full lips, not dissimilar to my own. Like most Nashwaltians, she is curvy, particularly around her hips, with a thin waist. The difference is generally that she wears a dull-coloured dress and always has her frizzy curls tied back, as per uniform. Unlike me, typically dressed in royal-coloured tulle and embroidered dresses, smothered in gold and pearl jewellery and expensive shoes. Hazel spends hours on my hair, braiding it into intricate patterns, often decorating it with freshly picked flowers and hand-made beads from the market, as is a common beauty custom in our country.

"Which shoes would you like to take with you, My Lady?" Hazel exhales, as though she's asked me a thousand times already.

"You pick," I tell her nonchalantly.

My lady-in-waiting makes an annoyed sound under her breath as she stuffs a gorgeous pair of heels, made of fine white lace and pink pearls, into the suitcase. She often chooses elegant things for me to wear. She knows my taste and knows that I prefer things that are feminine and elegant in nature. Clothing, at least.

"I knew you'd make a good choice," I flatter.

Hazel huffs in reply, clearly not amused by me. She makes a sound of strained effort to zip up the suitcase, which is bulging with the amount of clothing stuffed into it. Her hands are soft with thick fingers, not long and slender like mine. A testament to her love for pastries and other sweet treats. It's known in the kingdom that my lady-in-waiting, Hazel, enjoys many things in life, including sweets, travel and the attention of young men. That is why she has never been married.

"Those are lovely shoes," I tell Hazel.

"Well, it's only fair. You need to impress that Prince Fraviné, Your Highness," she replies with a sigh. "If he's going to ask for your hand, you'll need to look your best."

That is the reason I am headed to the secluded Island of Whŷstelkiné. My father insists that I marry Prince Fraviné, and become the Queen of Whŷstelkiné, a tiny seaside kingdom on an island in the middle of the Havvren sea. I have recently turned twenty-one, old enough to be married off to the man of highest status. Riches would help too. According to my father, Whŷstelkiné is a wealthy country, and Nashwalte could use more allies.

"That is true."

"And you will have some competition!"

Doubt washes over me with a little shiver in my shoulders. There is always the chance that the Prince of Whŷstelkiné has chosen another. There are many princesses and duchesses who would give anything to have a chance with a prince. I am simply one of dozens, and royal families can be ruthless. I've heard of royalty killing in the name of love, in the name of money, for a chance at marrying someone of a higher status.

The doubt must show on my face because Hazel adds kindly, "You'll look lovely, Your Highness. I have chosen your best dresses. The prince would have to be blind not to fall in love with you at first sight."

Her words do bring me some comfort, but there is still one thing that I worry about.

"I wish you were coming with me, Hazel."

"Oh, Princess! We've been over this, haven't we? You don't need me," Hazel insists. "You are perfectly capable of seducing that prince alone."

That is not true. I do need her. How will I tie my corset, or clip the clasps on my own dresses? My father is truly blind, not to understand that I need my lady-in-waiting for the simplest of tasks. The true reason that Hazel is refusing to come with me on this endeavour is because my father has already chosen the twelve staff required for the voyage. He has claimed that he needs more staff than I, and so my lady-in-waiting will be staying home, tending to the castle and my needs for when I return – hopefully with a marriage proposal from the prince, and a new castle for my lady-in-waiting and I to reside in.

"Now," Hazel says, picking up my suitcase by the handle

and heading towards the door to my large bedroom suite. "You only have a couple of hours before your voyage is due to commence. I shall assist you with your luggage. Let's go."

"I want you to come," I demand, decidedly.

Hazel's voice is firm when she tells me, "King Kelriaq has instructed me to stay, Your Highness. I will not refuse the directions of the king."

"Then I will."

By the time I find my father, there is only an hour left before the journey. King Kelriaq is drinking a mug of beer as he watches from the dock, while several servants heave his luggage onto his ship, that he affectionately calls *Sea Song*. He once fancied himself a brave man who travelled the seas alone. You'd hardly recognise him as such now, with his hundreds of servants.

My father's black, wiry beard barely rustles in the salty breeze as his dark eyes lock into place. He totally ignores my existence as I stride up to his side, my long braids and flowing dress streaming behind me.

"Father," I begin.

"Oh, Aruniar," he sighs, not taking his eyes off the ship. "Please do not nag. It is unbecoming."

"I didn't even say anything!"

"I know what you are going to ask."

"Oh?"

"You want to know why I won't allow your maid to join you for the voyage to the island." King Kelriaq has heard me complaining about the same things for at least a week now. Of course, he knows what I will say.

"I need her assistance." It's the same argument I've been making all week. "She helps me with all necessary tasks."

"What about my tasks, and my servants?"

"Surely you can make do with eleven servants, Father," I sigh. "Surely you can allow me one servant."

"There will be servants of the prince to assist you," the king argues.

"But they could also assist you!"

"Watch your tone, Princess."

"Please, Father. I need Hazel's assistance. I cannot do the simplest of tasks. How will I look my best for the prince? What if my hair is not done correctly, and he finds me repulsive?"

The king's expression changes. For the first time, his chocolate brown eyes turn from his ship to me, and I feel a glimmer of hope flutter in my chest. Perhaps I have finally gotten him to see my point. Perhaps his mind will change.

"You cannot even brush your own hair, my daughter?" His thick, black eyebrows raise quizzically.

"I can brush my hair, Father. I am not imbecilic. But how can I woo the prince without having my lady-in-waiting to make patterns and braid flowers in my hair? I need to win his attention over all other women if he is to marry me!"

"You think the prince will reject you over some hair?" The king does not look convinced.

"And my clothes," I add desperately. "It is impossible to tie your own corset, Your Majesty. Most of my dresses have clasps at the back. They are very difficult to fasten, without assistance."

The king strokes his unruly black beard with two fingers, his eyebrows furrowing and his brown eyes turning back to the ship.

It takes a little more convincing, but eventually my father says, "I suppose I could relieve my barber of his duties. We will only be gone a fortnight. How fast could my beard grow in that time?"

"Thank you!"

I hug him tightly, which is something my father has never been fond of. His arms are stiff and his body is warm as I embrace him for only a few short seconds.

"Now, Aruniar, remember she can only bring a single bag of luggage. She must be ready to set sail in less than an hour!" Now he's calling out to me as I rush back through the trees and bushes towards the track that leads to town.

Chapter 2

The air is salty and warm as I stand at the bow of the ship, looking down into the rushing waves. The sea foam below bubbles and fizzes as my father's ship cuts through the water, sending blue and green waves tumbling on either side of the massive vessel. It's as though the Havvren sea parts, making way for *Sea Song* and all who voyage upon it.

Birds soar high above the ship, wings outspread, gliding and calling shrilly to one another. They dive into the ocean, beak-first, wings tucked in. When the birds come back out of the waves, some have caught wriggling tiny silver fish in their beaks.

"My lady." Hazel is holding the skirt of her brown dress in one hand as she comes up by my side. "Your afternoon tea is ready. Would you like to come down to your cabin to have it?"

"No, I should like to drink my tea on the deck, thank you."

I'm still looking out to the diving birds. They barely make a splash as their aerodynamic bodies pierce the top of the ocean. It is breathtaking.

"It is far too hot out here, Your Highness," Hazel tells me. "Are you sure you wouldn't like to come out of the sun?"

"I'm sure."

"Very well," she breathes, her tone sounding as though she believes my attitude to be impossible. It is not an uncommon opinion. "I shall bring your tea, and perhaps your parasol?"

"That would be lovely."

When she's gone, I start to wonder about the Kingdom of

Whŷstelkiné. All I know of the island is what I have read in books from the Castle Library. It is a small island, hundreds of miles from any other land mass, with a small population of elves, not unlike me. Other than that, the island is a mystery.

When I attempted to ask my father about the island, all he offered was, "How can you expect me to have all of the answers?"

"You claim to have sailed far and wide!" I had reasoned stubbornly. "Surely you have been to Whŷstelkiné."

"I've journeyed to many lands! Whŷstelkiné is not one of them."

"Surely you have heard something about it! What is it like?" I had pressed.

"I understand it to be a small kingdom, with a lot of stories of the sea," my father had said, his tone turning dismissive and short. "I have heard that there are legends of sirens and sea monsters."

Legends of sea monsters. That sounds interesting. I wonder what kind of people make up stories about beasts of the sea. In fact, what kind of stories do they tell? I must admit that I am becoming very curious about this strange land and its secrets.

"Surely you know more," I press eagerly.

"Frewope, give me strength," my father says under his breath, looking out over the ocean.

There are two Nashwaltian gods. One of life and one of death. The Goddess of Life, Frewope the Devoted, believes in amity, perseverance and creativity. She is to blame for the creation of life and love, and all in between. She is responsible for the flowers that grow in the spring; Nashwalte babies born to gentle mothers; true love found in the most unlikely of places. And she is most generous to those who ask for her assistance.

Delrossa the Merciful is the God of Death. He is responsible for my mother's death and leading her into the Heavens. He is kind and charitable. He is compassionate. Delrossa the Merciful takes all those that are suffering. He places a gentle hand on their shoulder and leads them through a dark tunnel that leads to the velvet night sky. It is by his compassion and generosity that elves and animals alike have a second chance in the night sky.

When a seed is planted, Frewope the Devoted benevolently guides and nurtures the growing seed, and as the days pass, it develops into a beautiful rose. At the end of the season, as nature takes its course, the rose wilts and shrivels. Petals fall from the flower and the stem hardens. Seeing this, Delrossa the Merciful feels empathy in his heart. He caresses the flower and embraces it, so it may return to the Heavens, to be with the many other roses of the past.

This is how it has always been. This is how it shall always be.

Although one would think that the Goddess of Life and the God of Death are rivals or sworn enemies, their love story is quite the opposite. When the world was young, freshly created by Frewope, she was boastful. She claimed that Nashwalte would be the most beautiful of all the lands. For a long time, it was. With many trees and flowers, our country was alive with insects and other living creatures.

However, after some time, her creations began to wither and grow old. Despite her undeniable supremacy, the Goddess watched powerlessly as the trees and animals grew weak with illness. For many days and nights, Frewope, riddled with helplessness and depression, hid in the shadows of a cave.

That is when Delrossa, God of Death, came to her.

"I have watched your utopia from afar, and I watched the

beauty of your land fade with disease and old age," he told her. His voice was barely a whisper in the darkness of the shadowy cavern. "It must be painful to watch your creations suffer. I can help you."

Frewope the Devoted was no longer prideful. She was miserable. She was helpless. For the first time in her short life, she begged the God of Death to take her creations to the Heavens, and he did so with pleasure. In the following season, the trees and animals returned to their former beauty.

And while Frewope loved each of her creations, she knew that one day, Delrossa would give them a second life.

It would be three days' journey to the island of Whŷstelkiné. Three days until I meet my prince. Then I will have two weeks to seduce him. And two weeks to get my answers.

***

On the second day of travel, I sit on the deck of my father's ship, my head resting against the wooden railing. The blue sky turns with white clouds. Birds call. Apart from the lapping waves of the sea, it's the only sound that can be heard over the ocean. Their calls remind me of home.

For miles, there's nothing to see, but blue ocean, all the way to the flat line of the horizon. Occasionally, the pointed fin of a shark pierces the top of a wave, reminding me that although these waters look calm and still, there are hazards below. Perhaps not as exotic as legendary sea monsters, but predatory creatures, for certain.

The first day had been rough. It took me the longest time to find my sea-legs, and the motion of the ocean caused my stomach to heave with queasiness. The sickness swirled inside my gut for what felt like an eternity.

Hazel made me tea. She claimed that it would soothe my stomach. She knew all kinds of natural remedies; plants that cured headaches, weeds that counteracted the effects of poisons, teas that banned the influences of overindulgence of alcohol, roots that prevented diseases, smoke made of plants that ward off stinging insects. It was Old Medicine, and she knew all sorts. She had even taught me a few healing remedies, not that a princess had need of such things.

In fact, I believe that it why my father hired her as my lady-in-waiting in the first place. He believed that her knowledge of medicines would be able to cure me of any illness. I think that perhaps he was just nervous of my welfare after my mother unexpectedly died.

The tea had helped, and it wasn't long before I was up and about, insisting on a position on the deck, where I could see the ocean waves. Some of the servants have affectionately been calling me Sea Legs. I don't mind it; it's all in fun.

"Aruniar," my father says to me now, as I'm sitting on the warm wooden deck of the ship, looking up at the sky. "We have things to discuss. Things of import."

"What is it you'd like to discuss?" I ask him, my tone slightly bored as the hot sun causes sweat to bead on my forehead.

"Since you insisted that your lady-in-waiting come with us, it is your duty to ensure that she is safe," he instructs.

Whatever could that mean? Of course, she will be safe, and it is not as though King Kelriaq will not be there; he is standing right in front of me. He is the bravest and strongest man of Nashwalte. The Great King Kelriaq. He is also here on this journey. It is as much his duty as it is mine to ensure the safety of our servants.

"Father," I sigh. "Is this some sort of eccentric riddle you've made up?"

"Riddle?"

"Or, some kind of trick? An encryption?"

King Kelriaq's voice is becoming lurid and irritated when he demands, "Whatever are you talking about, Aruniar?"

"I do not understand what you mean," I tell him, exasperated.

"I mean that when travelling to other countries, there are obstacles." My father's tone is impatient, his gaze turning back to the ocean. "There are many threats, dangers. Although we are visiting this land and we must be respectful of their ways, we must also be wary."

"Of what?"

"Of others!"

"Speak plainly, Father."

"Your lady-in-waiting is your concern. Should anything happen to her, you should be solely responsible."

As my father walks away from me, I turn back towards the sky. Already, I kind of miss my home. I miss my bed. I miss a world that doesn't rock with ocean waves. I miss my cat, Jipperiya.

Part of me wishes to go home already. Deep inside me is a question of whether this journey is worth it; what if the kingdom is undesirable? What if the prince I am supposed to marry is unfriendly or hostile? What if he does not find me attractive?

I think myself into a frenzy on the deck of the ship, my anxieties eating me up from the inside out. My worries make me feel ill again. Inside my stomach, I feel a churning that pains my bones.

As if summoned by my thoughts, my lady-in-waiting, appears at my side, holding a teacup. She holds the cup out to me, her expression closed and unreadable.

"How are you feeling, Your Highness?" Hazel asks.

"A little dizzy." As I sip the tea that she's given me, the sickness in my belly subsides. "A bit better now. Thank you."

"Of course."

Chapter 3

The sky is warm with splashes of orange and pink, sunlight reflecting off the sea, as *Sea Song* approaches Whŷstelkiné. In the distance, I see tall mountains, a rocky shore, waves crashing against a massive cliff face, where a grey castle sits perched atop, overlooking the ocean. The tall towers made of grey stone on either side of the castle remind me of a story I once heard about a stolen baby.

As the ship approaches, a town beside the castle comes into view. There are buildings made of stone a similar colour to that of the sharp rocks below the cliff face. Grey, with a tinge of blue. Atop the buildings, flags of blue and white flap in the wind.

A feeling of dread overwhelms me. I feel it rise in my stomach, twist in my chest.

What if this endeavour fails? What if the prince rejects me? What is this was all for nothing?

Fear strikes my heart and suddenly I feel woozy.

"Princess," Hazel starts, her firm hand on my shoulder as I sit directly on the deck of the ship, the warm timber hard on my buttocks. "What is the matter?"

"I feel faint," I tell her quietly, so not to make a fuss.

"I shall return with some water."

While she is disappearing beneath the deck of the ship, I watch the island get closer and closer. I watch the sharp rocks grow larger and more fearsome.

Sea Song steers around the side of the island, quickly, but not unsteadily. There is a small bay on the east side of the island, where several large fishing boats are docked, tied lazily to trees and timber poles dug deep into the sand. A couple of smaller boats, only big enough to be paddled, accompany the fishing boats, not tied but simply strewn upon the hot, red sand.

Who would leave their boat like this?

It seems strange that for a small island kingdom, so fascinated by the sea – to go as far as to make up stories of sea monsters – there is no port. How do they import supplies? How do they contact other lands?

The sand is hot. It burns the bottoms of my feet as I hop to the end of the bay, where tall trees with fat leaves, cast a wide shadow on the sand for me to stand upon, while I wait for the crew to unload my luggage. In the trees, there are fruits the size of my fist, pink in colour, with yellow prickles on the skin.

Part of me wants to pick the fruit. I want to taste it and see what kinds of wonders and secrets this island hides. Just as I'm about to reach for it, it occurs to me that I have never seen this fruit before.

What if it's poisonous? Why else would it have thorns? It is probably a warning.

I watch as my father's servants stand at various locations on the ship, throwing luggage to each other. Each suitcase, bag, and box are caught, then passed to another servant. I watch the production line, passing the luggage from one person to the next, each caught with a strained noise, before thrown to the next servant. The luggage lands in a pile on the red sand, just beside the ship.

"Your Highness!"

Hazel comes down the stairs and walks right across the sand and shells to me. In one hand, she holds the skirt of her dress, and in the other she is holding a pair of brown sandals with long straps in her hand. She's looking at me with a cross expression.

"Your feet must be burning!" she exclaims in disbelief. "Please put these on, Your Highness."

"I'm fine, Hazel," I dismiss, although the soles of my feet are quite sore. Perhaps I will get blisters. "I shall stay in the shade for now."

"You have no idea what kinds of fauna and flora we may come across on this island!" Hazel lectures. "What if an insect stings you? How will we know if you are allergic, or if it is lethal? Please wear the shoes, Your Highness, for my sake."

"Fine."

I put on the leather sandals that she holds out to me, just hoping that it will shut her up. I twist the straps up my calf and tie a bow in the side.

"Happy?" I ask her with a sigh.

"Ecstatic."

A yell from the ship catches my attention. I look up just in time to see a floral suitcase being thrown overboard. It lands with a firm *thunk* in the blue water. Just like that, it is soaked through, sinking heavily to the bottom of the bay. I watch helplessly as lapping waves push my suitcase up onto the hot sand. Shells and broken coral make a brittle, crackling sound under the weight of my luggage.

"Oh no!" Hazel gasps. "Now, Your Highness. Please don't worry…"

But I am not listening. I run across the shore to my suitcase and kneel beside it, my dress now dipping into the cool lapping waves as I desperately unzip the suitcase. Inside, I see that all my clothes are soaked. Tulle and lace hang from my dresses, torn and broken, as I take them out one by one, and place them on the sand beside me. They are ruined. Not a thing survived the seawater.

At first, it is anger I feel seething in my throat. Then, it turns to worry.

What will I do without my elegant dresses to woo the prince? How will I seduce him without the delicate fabrics and expensive jewels? What will set me apart from the other princesses and duchesses who desire his attention?

"Your Highness, please don't be alarmed," Hazel pants, having sprinted up behind me and now leaning over to catch her breath. "We shall fix this."

"How can I not be alarmed? How can we fix this?" I shout, but my voice betrays me as it quivers.

"We will buy you new dresses," she tells me evenly. "Your father will understand. I will find you a dressmaker, the finest in Whŷstelkiné. I swear it! Now, come with me. I'll get you cleaned up. We can't have the prince seeing you like this for the first time. We must make an impression!"

She is right. The skirt of my pink dress is soaked through, my buttocks and legs plastered in wet, red sand. Warm, salty water drips down my cheeks and neck, sticking whisks of curly hair to my face and running down my shoulders. I cannot meet the Prince of Whŷstelkiné for the first time looking like this! He would be appalled and would certainly discard me.

Dejectedly, I follow Hazel back onto the ship. Inside my cabin, Hazel dries my hair and face with a warm cotton towel. She wraps the towel around my shoulders tenderly.

"You must be cold," she tells me.

When I don't reply, she says, "It was not very bright of you to rush into that water, Princess. We don't know these waters. There could have been sharks or jellyfish. You could have been hurt!"

"I'm fine, Hazel."

If my mother were here, she would scold me for using such a tone with Hazel, my trusted friend and advisor. She would tell me to be grateful. But, sometimes, it is hard to be grateful when you are constantly being scolded.

"Next time, I shall assist you. Do not go running into unknown waters yourself. You could have been hurt."

"I'm not hurt," I insist, annoyance tingling my throat, my tone rising. "I'm fine!"

"It is dangerous!"

I sigh. It is pointless to argue with my lady-in-waiting. She is stubborn and bossy, but she cares about me. She is kind of like a mother – if a mother were only a year older than me.

Hazel wrings out my dress, catching the water in a bucket, and I use my hairbrush to comb the tangles out of my long hair. My hair smells of salt and sand. It is awful. As I brush my hair, I notice that there is a small piece of seaweed tangled in it.

"Oh, Princess!" Hazel says in a frustrated voice. "See, this is why you cannot go into the sea!"

"Okay," I mumble uselessly. "I get it."

Once my dress is as wringed out as it is going to get, and Hazel has fashioned my still-damp hair into a row of traditional Nashwaltian braids, we head back out of the cabin. I follow Hazel to the stairs, and she holds my hand so that I don't fall. When we step back onto the beach, my sandalled foot sinks into shallow water. The tide has come up a little since *Sea Song* anchored.

The red sand is now cold, as the sun has sunk below the horizon, swallowed up by the blue ocean, replaced by a shining white crescent moon. Hundreds of stars twinkle amongst the velvet sky. My mother smiles down at me from Heaven.

King Kelriaq and his servants are waiting at the edge of the beach. Many servants are sitting on trunks and suitcases, chatting and laughing amongst themselves, while the king leans against a tall tree with a mug of beer in his hand. He's watching me closely, a closed expression on his face.

"I heard about your suitcase," he says flatly as I approach him. "It's a real shame."

"A shame indeed," Hazel nods sympathetically as she pats my hand. "She will need new dresses, Your Majesty, if she is to impress the prince."

"I'm afraid you are right," my father sighs. "Surely you, Hazel, will find a dressmaker tomorrow in the town square?"

"Of course, Sire." Hazel's voice is accommodating. "I would be honoured."

"Very good."

Warm yellow lights of the kingdom glow in the distance, as we make our way through the mangroves and light forest. There is a narrow path, made of rocks and sand, that leads us through the trees and towards the kingdom. Upon reaching the gates, King Kelriaq sends a squire ahead to introduce the King and Princess of Nashwalte, while the rest of us wait at the end of the forest.

Standing at the open gate, the entire town seems to be made of the grey stone, aside from the roads which are only made of red sand. The straight road, which seems to hold the entire kingdom, leads directly to the grey stone castle, where there is a staircase and heavy, wooden doors.

Within a few minutes, much of the town has gathered just inside the kingdom gates to welcome us. I cast my eyes over the hundreds of people gathered here, my heart thrumming in my chest.

Movement at the top of the stairs to the castle catches my

eye as a woman in a red dress, who I presume to be the Queen of Whŷstelkiné, exits the wooden door. She stands stationary, leaning against a gold staff, a jewelled crown glinting upon her head.

Behind her, the door opens again and a tall, thin man steps into view. His golden hair glimmers in the yellow hue of the streetlamps surrounding.

"That must be the prince," Hazel whispers to me, tapping my arm excitedly. "Is it love at first sight?"

Well, it's hard to tell.

He's so far away. I can't really see him from where I'm standing. I'm going to need to get much closer to tell whether I'm in love with him or not. I might also need a bit more time.

"Um," I mumble.

Just then, King Kelriaq enters the gates. He takes long, assured strides, looking out at the crowd as he marches confidently towards the castle. His shiny, black shoes reflect the light of the moon and make a soft chuffing sound on the red sand below.

I wait a moment, before I follow him, leaving a decent gap between us so that we have time to be announced to the Royal Family of Whŷstelkiné when we finally get to the end.

As I walk, I feel the whole town looking at me. Hundreds of pairs of eyes staring at me. Their eyes are starting to bore into me, as though they're burning holes into my body. I'm starting to feel uncomfortable, which is strange, because much of my life has required public speaking and having hundreds of eyes on me. For some reason, there's something different about it this time.

Looking around at the sea of people that surround me, I notice that they look different. Although they have pointed ears like mine, their hair is like that of the prince: hues of golden and yellow. Their skin is a lighter tone than mine, beige like the deer back home.

"Who is she?" I hear them whispering to each other. "What is she doing here?"

It makes my stomach twist and my heart skip to know that hundreds of people are looking at me and asking questions. It makes me question my being here. Perhaps I could just run the rest of the way, get this over with. I'm starting to feel nervous as I approach halfway.

My father looks left and right as he walks through the crowded street, waving royally to anyone and everyone. He's got a confident smile on his face.

How I wish I was as confident as he. How I wish I wasn't feeling so nervous. How I wish...

Suddenly, I notice that there are several people in the crowd waving to me. There are many children sitting atop parents' shoulders, waving with both hands, calling out to me. A little girl with yellow pig tails and a tattered dress stumbles out into the road, her little white feet a stark contrast to the red sand.

I stop. I look down at her for a moment, unsure what to do, until a wide smile cracks her face.

"Hi!" I crouch beside her, all of my weight on the balls of my feet as I reach a hand out to her. To my surprise, she takes it in her firm grasp. "I'm Princess Aruniar. What's your name?"

"Are you really a princess?" Her eyes, bluer than any I've ever seen, are wide in amazement.

"Yes," I tell her with a smile.

"Are you going to marry Prince Frąviné?" she asks me.

"I hope so!"

A thin young woman with gold ringlets steps forward out of the crowd and gives me what I think is an embarrassed smile, whispering an apology. Her pea-green eyes shine in the moonlight as she takes the little girl's hand and leads her daughter back off the street. A moment later, mother and daughter are standing in the crowd, the little girl waving at me from the young woman's arms.

I continue down the sandy road, keeping eyes up, confidence growing in my chest after my encounter with the little girl who was so excited to meet me. As I walk the rest of the way to the castle, I feel my heart fluttering, with, not nerves now, but exhilaration. For a moment, I allow myself to imagine what it could be like to rule this tiny kingdom, with that little girl waving at me each day as I walk through the streets.

"Queen Nyssra of Whŷstelkiné, may I present King Kelriaq of Nashwalte," the squire calls in a loud voice to the crowd from atop the grey stairs, as my father approaches the bottom stair.

I watch my father take delicate steps, his shoes scuffing softly on the stone, his cape puffing with each upwards stride. He bows to the queen when they're standing face to face, and Queen Nyssra curtsies in response, pulling her red dress slightly aside. Beside her, Prince Frąviné bows his head to King Kelriaq.

"May I present Princess Aruniar of Nashwalte," the squire announces loudly.

Looking up from where I stand at the bottom of the grey stone steps, my eyes lock onto Prince Frąviné's, and the edge of his top lip curls slightly. The first thing I notice about him is that his skin is the shade of wheat in a field. He has freckled cheeks, straight blond hair tied in a ponytail that reaches past his shoulders. Sitting atop his head, he has a diadem of gold-painted seashells. A single shell on a black cord hangs around his neck. He wears a white shirt, only half-buttoned, that hangs loosely from him, as though it were a size too large for his athletic figure.

I take a slow and deliberate step as I start up the stairs. The stone is a little slippery beneath my brown sandal, but I take a deep breath to steady myself and slowly climb the stairs, all the while keeping my gaze on the prince.

When I reach the top of the stairs, Prince Frąviné is the first to bow. He dips low, before he reaches a light-toned hand, plastered with freckles, out. His fingers are warm as they hold mine. His lips gently brush my knuckles, and then his sapphire eyes lock onto mine and I feel my stomach do a backflip.

"Lovely to meet you, Aruniar," the prince says in a soft voice as he stares deep into my eyes. His voice is heavy with a thick accent I've never heard before. It rings in my head, so that I must focus to understand his words. "I have waited for this day."

"As have I," I reply, matching his quiet tone.

When I stand before the queen, she bows her head to me and I offer a deep curtsey, keeping my head low.

"Welcome to my home," Queen Nyssra greets warmly. "Please come in. I have a servant arranging the East Wing for you as we speak. We'll have supper while we wait."

"Thank you," my father replies politely, before he follows Queen Nyssra and Prince Frąviné into the castle. "That would be wonderful."

Chapter 4

Upon entering the stone castle, the first thing I notice is that there is a large portrait of the royal family hung on the wall of the entryway. The family is much larger than I expected. Featured in the portrait is the king, queen and not just Prince Frąviné, but five other young princes, who all look very similar.

All family members portrayed in the painting have golden hair and pale skin. Three princes have curls like Nyssra, while the other three, including Frąviné, have straight locks, like their father's. All the family wears shells as jewellery. There are bracelets, necklaces, anklets and crowns made of various shells and dried-up seahorses. I wonder whether shells are like riches in this country.

This portrait was painted long ago. I can tell because not only is Prince Frąviné much shorter, appearing to be the same height as his mother, but one of the young princes is a baby in Queen Nyssra's arms.

King Kelriaq makes small talk with Queen Nyssra as they walk together through the large entry and into what I assume is the ballroom, with a shiny polished hard-wood floors and hanging crystal chandeliers that twinkle with white light.

"Do you have many balls back home?" The prince wants to know.

"Not many," I tell him, still taking in the beautiful room. "Only on special occasions. I had a ball for my birthday this year when I turned twenty-one. Most of the kingdom came."

"Even peasants?"

The word 'peasant' takes me by surprise. So much that I find myself making a soft gasping sound. My father believes 'peasant' to be a slur for people less fortunate than us. I have never heard the term used so casually before.

Prince Fraviné, however, seems unfazed by my sudden noise, so I try to pretend that it didn't happen as I regain my composure.

"Yes. Even those of low status." I speak very slowly and evenly, choosing my words and tone carefully. "Do you host many balls?"

"Not as many as I would like," the prince says regretfully. "I would like to throw parties all the time, but my mother does not like them so much. She gets very tired these days, you see. She and my father used to host many balls when I was young, but she's getting old."

"I understand."

The queen opens another large wooden door and leads my father through it. The prince and I follow.

In this room there are large couches, with blue cushions and gold trim. There is the name of the island embroidered in gold onto one of the couch cushions. A thick white and gold rug, that squishes softly under my feet, sits on the hardwood floor between the two couches.

On the stone wall behind the furniture, a blue and white flag is pinned up. Upon closer inspection, now that I have a moment to examine it, I discern that the flag of Whŷstelkiné depicts a strange snake-like creature, slithering in white across the blue background of the flag. The snake does not appear to have scales, but barbed thorns that protrude from all angles of its slender body.

While Queen Nyssra slowly and carefully takes a seat on one of the couches, the prince sits on the other. Both elegantly cross their legs at the knee. As they sit before me, their mannerisms nearly identical, I take a moment to appreciate their similarities; Fraviné has Nyssra's long, slender nose, her pointed chin and high cheekbones, thin lips that form a serious line across his features.

My father sits beside the queen, and I sit alongside Prince Fraviné, who looks delighted that I chose to sit beside him. His white teeth shine in the bright light of the sitting room and his blue eyes practically glint with happiness.

"Would you host many balls, if you could?" the prince asks me. "You enjoy them, no?"

"Yes, I enjoy balls," I answer with a smile. "I think the novelty could wear off if I hosted them all the time though. I understand that Queen Nyssra may have grown tired of them."

"I suppose." His voice is soft when he says it, his demeanour completely changed from earlier.

"Your tea, Your Majesty." A thin servant with blond hair and a mole on his nose bows low as he holds out a tiny teacup to the queen.

Another servant offers Prince Fraviné and my father a cup of tea, who both take the cup gratefully.

"Your tea, Your Highness," the servant with the mole – whose name I know now to be Grithoné – says to me as he comes back to the couch.

"Thank you," I reply in a soft voice.

As I look down at my teacup, I notice that the tea smells like a garden of roses. I am surprised to see that the tea is a light shade of pink, with tiny specks of white floating on the top of the liquid. The steam that rises from the cup is warm and floral, a slightly pink tinge, as it touches my nostrils.

"You seem intrigued by the tea," the prince observes, appearing amused. "Do you have tea where you are from?"

"Yes," I answer, although I'm a little embarrassed to be caught staring at a cup of liquid. "Our tea is made of leaves and mint."

"That sounds refreshing!"

"What is this tea made from?" I ask curiously.

"Well, I'm not sure," the prince tells me, a confused smile creeping onto his thin pink lips. "I've never asked. Perhaps I could call a servant back and get them to tell you if you like?"

"No, no need to bother them. I'm sure they're very busy."

A look of surprise crosses Prince Fraviné's face, his gold eyebrows turning lopsided as one raises, and one furrows. His blue eyes are sturdy on mine when he tells me firmly, "My servants are never too busy for my princess."

Just then, my lady-in-waiting joins us in the sitting room. She comes directly to me and stands beside the blue velvet couch that I am sitting on.

"Oh, Prince Fraviné, this is my lady-in-waiting, Hazel," I introduce them, taking my first sip of the pink tea in my hand. It's surprisingly sweet and tickles the tip of my tongue with both the heat and the sweetness of it.

"Charmed," Hazel greets politely.

The prince's face is unreadable as he looks at Hazel, his mouth still a serious, straight line that matches his mother's.

"She is very good," I assure him. "She takes good care of me."

"As she should," the prince replies simply, now looking my lady-in-waiting up and down. "She can be replaced."

Hazel's light brown eyes widen, and her mouth slackens

with shock. I feel her looking at me for assistance, but I don't look back at her, for fear of Prince Frąviné believing that I am surprised – which I am, but I don't want him to know that. Perhaps he will judge me and my country.

Remember, Aruniar, we are here to make an alliance.

"Do you have a personal servant, Your Highness?" I try to redirect the conversation.

"It's 'Your Royal Highness'. And, yes, I have a lord-in-waiting," Prince Frąviné replies, holding the teacup to his mouth, but not sipping it. "In fact, I have several. One could not be enough for the assistance I need."

"Yes, I understand. They have many responsibilities, don't they? I am lucky to have such a helpful and knowledgeable lady-in-waiting."

"Indeed." Prince Frąviné's voice changes when he says this, and his eyes turn cold as he looks from me to Hazel.

I wait for him to add more, but no more is added. He simply tips up his cup and drinks the entire cup of tea in one mouthful. When he is done, without asking or waiting for the offer, he places the teacup in Hazel's hand and looks at her expectantly, until she leaves the room. I watch her confoundedly take the cup to the servant with the mole, who has been waiting by the door.

As I watch my lady-in-waiting scurry away, a feeling of irritation rises in me. I don't realise that I am scowling, until I make eye-contact with the prince, who is staring at me in a way that is disconcerting. It makes my skin tickle with discomfort, but I offer him a polite smile, in hopes that it will conjure a more emotive expression from him.

Then his intense gaze moves, sliding up from my eyes, over my forehead, to my hair, where my tiara, bejewelled with white pearls, sits upon my head. His eyes narrow, a muscle in his jaw twitching slightly.

"What an interesting crown." He says it so plainly, so apathetically, that I almost think I have imagined it.

"It was my mother's," I reply.

He blinks, expression almost bored. Finally, his eyes flick to mine, and he says, "You shan't wear it in my kingdom."

I am in such disbelief that I cannot even think of a reply. I cannot believe what he has said. All I can do is sit there with my jaw nearly on the floor.

"Right, well, I guess I shall be heading off to bed then," the prince says suddenly. He abruptly stands from the couch and adjusts his hair. "I shall be seeing you, my princess."

He kisses my hand one last time, before he strides out of the sitting room, closing the heavy wooden door firmly behind him.

I stare after him, his words still repeating in my head.

Who has the nerve to say something like that to a stranger?

"Shall I draw you a bath, Your Highness?" Hazel offers when she returns to my side, where I have been left with Queen Nyssra and my father, who are too deep in conversation to notice that the prince has left.

"Yes, please, Hazel," I answer. "I believe we are staying in the East Wing."

"I shall take you to your room, Princess Aruniar."

I follow my lady-in-waiting through the ballroom, up a magnificent staircase, lined with white carpet, and a cross a long balcony with a gold railing. My chambers are on the left side of the corridor, behind a heavy wooden door with a shiny gold doorknob.

When I enter my room, Hazel helps me to undo my dress and corset before she runs a hot bubble bath in my attached bathroom.

In my unfastened dress, my tiara now placed on the dressing table, I stand on a balcony that overlooks the roaring sea outside, while I wait for my bath to be ready. The wind is cool as it blows back my hair and fills my lungs with salty air. I see white stars high above, and the moon glowing brilliantly. It occurs to me that I can be so far from home, and yet the night sky still appears the same.

Chapter 5

Below my window, there is a mysterious sound. A whistling. It reminds me of the birdsong from the forests outside my bedroom back home. The pitch is a high, musical note.

Standing on my balcony, looking over the sea, the cool breeze twists and blows my black curls from my shoulders. Trying to see over the side of the balcony, I rest my weight on my palms as I lean over the stone railing. There's a green, slimy moss that covers the stones, and my hand slips slightly. The stone grazes the skin of my wrist. A few drops of blood rise to the surface of my skin. I squint at it in the dim light that streams out of my chambers.

Then there's a more distinct whistle. This one is bright and clear, compared to the musical whistling that seems to echo over the ocean.

"Princess?" comes a familiar man's voice from the darkness below.

"Yes?" I call back.

"You look lovely," the voice calls to me.

As I look down at myself, I suddenly remember that I have already bathed and am only wearing bed clothes; a silky nightdress and sheer robe – both items that my lady-in-waiting managed to find in the castle while I was having a hot bath – that barely hides a thing! I make a high-pitched sound of surprise and pull the robe tightly against my body.

"No, my princess, I truly mean it." The prince's face appears just below the stone railing, enough light on his face for me to recognise him. "You are stunning."

He is holding the stone wall with his large, pale hands. Although his fingertips are white with the grip he holds on the stone, his shoulders and arms do not shake. He is not wearing a shirt, but just a pair of loose shorts, the elastic tight around the lower side of his hips, exposing his muscular arms and smooth chest.

I wonder whether I am staring when I say, "Thank you."

There is silence between us for a moment, and I spend the entire three seconds trying not to look at his hairless body.

"What are you doing out here so late?" I ask him.

"I was going for a brisk evening walk," he explains, still holding onto the wall and grinning at me, his blue eyes drilling into mine. "Would you like to accompany me?"

"I'm hardly dressed for a walk, Your Highness."

"Neither am I!" he beams. "Do you see that stopping me?"

"I suppose not."

"Come on then," he urges.

Then I watch Prince Fraviné climb back down the railing. His toned arms glisten in the light from my chambers as he climbs, moving with such agility that I almost imagine that he walked directly out of my dreams. He disappears into the darkness below without a sound.

For a moment, I consider going back into my chambers and slamming the door. I would hide under the covers, and stay there forever.

I am humiliated. I cannot imagine facing the prince again now that he has seen me in nothing but my nightdress! Not a corset or gown in sight! He could probably see right through my dress!

But from beneath the balcony, I hear him call, "Princess!"

His voice is smooth like butter, and I feel my stomach twist. As I look over the railing, my heart skips a beat and I feel my blood racing in my veins. It's too dark to see if he is down there, but the thought of him gazing at me from below is enough to make my cheeks burn.

"Yes?" I squeak.

"Well, are you coming?"

"Okay."

Cautiously, I hold the railing with both hands, so not to slip on the moss and green gunk and swing one leg over the balcony to follow him down the side of the stone wall. The grey stone is cold under my legs. It makes a cool shiver trickle down my spine.

"Do you need help?" Prince Fṛaviné shouts to me from under the balcony.

I feel a rush of fear tickle my stomach.

What if I fall? How far is this balcony from the ground? Is it far? Will I be hurt if I fall?

Suddenly, a warm hand is wrapped around my ankle. A shriek escapes me.

Let Delrossa take me now!

"Princess!" the prince speaks in a hushed tone. His fingers are gentle on my foot, and I'm overly aware of how warm they feel. "It's just me. I'll help you."

"It's too far," I gasp. "I'm going back!"

"Trust me. I've got you."

Slowly, I inch closer to the end of the railing. Now both of my legs are over the side and Prince Fṛaviné takes both of my feet in his grasp. He instructs me on how to get off the balcony, then he catches me in his arms as I free-fall from the railing. His warm arms wrap around my waist as he holds me against his body.

"Told you I had you," he whispers against my ear.

The prince holds me in his arms for a moment longer, as though I weigh nothing, weightless in his strength. Then, he puts me down so that my feet are touching the damp grass, and he takes my hand in his.

"It's dark out here. I'll lead you, until your eyes adjust," Prince Fṛaviné tells me. "Follow me."

He leads me under the balcony, his clasp firm on my fingers. As we walk along the tree line of the cliff-face, the smell of salt pervades my senses and the cool breeze blows my silky night-dress.

We walk soundlessly together for a few minutes. The shining crescent moon glows peacefully above, the ocean waves crash on the rocky cliff-face and in the distance, there is a soft whistling of birdsong. I feel my eyes adjusting to the darkness, but I don't ask the prince to release his grip on my hand.

Eventually, we come to a rocky surface that overlooks the ocean. The tide laps at the shiny, flat rocks and the reflection of the moon ripples on the water. The water is so clear that I can see several silver fish whirling beneath the surface.

I watch as Prince Fṛaviné takes a seat on the rocks, crossing his legs under his body and tucking his feet under his knees. He pats the empty space beside him.

"Sit with me."

But… the rocks are wet.

They glisten with dampness. I'll get my night-dress wet. I'll have to go to bed in wet clothes – or sleep without any clothes!

My thoughts must show on my face because the prince laughs. "You don't have to sit down if you don't want to. But you'll be uncomfortable if you stand there the whole time we're here."

We look at each other and I sigh.

"Fine."

As I take a seat on the flat rock next to him, I feel the bitter moisture from the rock seep through my nightdress. It's cold on my skin. I shiver.

When I look at the prince, he is gazing across the ocean. His eyes appear far away, kind of hazy. Distracted. Unfocussed. As though he is deep in thought.

What is he thinking about?

"My father used to take me here," he tells me quietly.

"Your father?"

"The King Dijphozạạ."

"Oh."

"We used to take that sailboat down there." He gestures, but in the darkness, I can't see where he points. "We couldn't go past the reef, but he'd take me out on the water sometimes. He showed me how to sail. My brothers too. We all know."

"Wow, that is an important skill!"

"He died when I was a kid," Prince Frạviné goes on, talking to the ocean. "He fell ill. He was older than my mother, and he was unwell. His heart couldn't take any more."

Gently, I slide my hand onto his. "Oh, that's horrible. I'm so sorry."

"It was a long time ago."

"How old were you?"

"Thirteen," Prince Frạviné answers simply. He answers quickly. He doesn't need to think about it; the memory is seared into his mind.

A glossiness comes over his sapphire eyes. His lips are a firm line as he stares over the ocean, the wind rustling his blond hair. In the silence, it is blaringly obvious that I can't think of anything useful to say.

"It's nice out here," I offer.

"We would fish here. It was our spot."

"Yeah?"

"Yeah," the prince breathes. Then his expression changes and there's a mischievous glint in his eyes when he adds, "One time, I caught a huge salmon! I swear it was this big" – he holds his hands two feet apart – "and my father was so proud! He taught me how to fillet it, and we took it home."

"Really? The King of Whŷstelkiné could fillet some salmon?"

"Yeah! Amazing, right?" There's an amused tone that comes over Prince Frąviné's voice and he finally turns to me. "My mother was so angry when I walked into the castle with it! I cooked it in the kitchen, and she refused to eat any of it. She was convinced that it would make us sick."

"Did it?"

"No. My youngest brother is allergic to salmon, but he wasn't born yet."

"I saw the portrait of your family in the castle," I add.

"Yeah." He nods. Now he's leaning back on his hands. "My mother loves that picture. I guess it's the last one she has of my father before he died. Sometimes, I catch her staring at it late at night."

"She must miss him."

"She must."

"You have a lot of brothers," I observe, recalling the identical faces in the painting.

The prince laughs. "Five brothers is a lot."

"Are you the oldest?"

"The second oldest. My older brother, Vrenïmq, was involved in an unfortunate accident," Prince Frąviné explains vaguely. His tone is flat, emotionless as he stares out at the sea. "He died last year."

"I'm sorry."

He shrugs. "Four brothers left."

The comment catches me off-guard, and I stare at the prince's face briefly.

"Anyway," Prince Frąviné sighs, now standing and brushing off his shorts. "I guess I'd better get back to my chambers. If my mother notices that I'm missing, she might have some things to say about it."

"Would she notice?"

"Perhaps," the prince sighs, offering me a hand up. "Sometimes, she stops by my younger brothers' chambers to check on them while they sleep. And sometimes we chat late at night."

I'm struck by the sensitive tone that he uses when speaking about his mother. His affection for her.

"You and your mother are close?" I ask.

We head back in the direction of the castle. I follow him very closely, my bare feet slipping a little on the rocks.

"Oh, very." Prince Frąviné nods. "She is my greatest friend."

"Really?"

"She was very lonely when my father died," the prince begins to explain. "She needed me and my older brother when my father passed, and even more so when we discovered that she was pregnant a year later."

The last part causes me to question a few things, but I don't dare say them aloud. I would not interrogate the prince about his mother's integrity. That kind of accusation could bring a lot of shame to a family, especially one with such high status. And besides, it could be a mistake.

"Thank you for sharing so much with me tonight," I say when we arrive back on the balcony outside my chambers. "That would have been hard for you."

The prince holds my hands in his as he looks into my eyes. The corner of his mouth twitches into a crooked smile and I totally forget about the first impression I had of the prince earlier tonight.

Perhaps he is not the pompous jerk that I believed him to be. Perhaps he is misunderstood. Perhaps he is kind and romantic, under that stoic, rude demeaner.

He certainly has been through a lot.

Slowly, Prince Frąviné leans forward and places a soft kiss on my cheek. His thin, supple lips are delicate and cool against my flushed skin.

"Good night, my princess," he whispers to me.

"Good night."

Perhaps, he is not as bad as he seems.

Chapter 6

The heat here is dissimilar to home. Unlike Nashwalte, the weather here is a sort of heat that doesn't hang around your body; you simply sweat the heat out, and your body returns to normal when the doors are closed. Back home, the humidity of the rainforest sticks to one's skin. It suffocates the pores. Even sweat has trouble seeping out of you before the rains come.

When I awake the next morning, I am reminded of the fact that I am no longer in Nashwalte. In fact, there is a chance I will never return there, if I can convince the prince to marry me.

Hazel is speaking to me in a gentle voice. Her warm hand is on my shoulder as she speaks to me closely, droning about dresses and a seamstress she's found in the town square.

When I open my eyes, I see her face close to mine, as she whispers close to my ear, "We must go now, Your Highness. We don't want anyone to see that you are wearing the same clothes as yesterday. Here, let me help you dress."

She pulls the covers off me, places my corset around my waist and tightens the drawstrings until I must suck in my stomach a little for that hourglass look. My lady-in-waiting helps me fasten the clips on the same pink dress from yesterday and while she is tying my braids into a quick bun at the back of my head, I pull on my brown sandals, which are still slightly damp from walking into the water when the tide had come in.

We walk quickly through the castle, avoiding any servants who are bringing coffee and breakfast to our hosts. I follow Hazel as she heads straight through the front door of the castle and into the sunlight.

Out in the street, I see the town for the first time in the daylight; the sandy road is a vibrant red, littered with yellow and white rocks the size of my fingernail. There are small patches of grass on either side of the road, but mostly it is scarlet dust and dirt that secures the road and buildings in place. Each building is made of the same grey-blue stone. Lamps and dated wooden signs hang from the outsides of the buildings, swinging noisily in the light wind that rustles leaves in tall nearby trees with strange pink fruits.

There are merchants in the street, with tiny wooden stalls, selling fruit, flowers, fabrics, and beads. As we walk along the road, I hear some bartering and chatting. It reminds me of home, the sound of trading in our town square, when I go with Hazel to run errands or be fitted for new clothes.

As we pass the buildings, I take note of the kinds of stores I would like to come back to when we are not in such a rush. We pass a shoemaker and a fish market. There are several bakeries and even a furniture store, with handmade wooden tables and chairs out the front.

Hazel ducks into the next building, through a heavy wooden door with a window in the centre. Above the door reads a wooden sign: *Pénquil the Modiste.*

The door makes a jingling sound that startles me, as it closes and shuts heavily as the lock clicks into place. Inside the shop, it smells of lavender and honey, a strange, yet comforting combination. The lights in the dressmaker's shop are a dim yellow, only illuminating enough for me to see outlines of objects to begin with, before my eyes adjust to the darkness.

Now that I can see, there are dozens of mannequins, some

by the shop window, but most scattered throughout the shop. Each mannequin wears an exquisite dress, of all different colours and luxurious fabrics.

My feet stop walking, and I admire a skin-tight dress made of red velvet and black trim. This dress is shorter than I would usually wear, the skirt only coming to the mannequin's mid-thigh, with a slit up the left side that stops a finger's length below the hip. The neck of the dress is a deep V that dips low into the chest, revealing more cleavage than I even knew was legal.

This dress is provocative!

It is erotic, and I can't help imagining myself wearing it.

"What do you think?" A voice with a thick accent like the prince's makes me jump.

When I turn to look at the person speaking to me, I notice that it is a young woman who is slightly taller than me, with a gentle smile and freckled cheeks. A similar appearance to all those who live in Whŷstelkiné, her hair is wavy and blond, eyes are as green as leaves and her light skin nearly glows next to mine. What surprises me most is that she is not dressed in dull colours, but in a royal blue dress stitched to black floral lace. She must be a duchess!

"The dresses are beautiful," I tell her admiringly. "If a little provocative."

"Provocative?" She gestures to the red velvet dress before us. "This dress? Please, you haven't seen provocative yet, Your Highness, I assure you."

"It is more sensual than what I would wear, that is for sure. That dress suggests that the wearer is promiscuous, which I am not."

"What would you wear?"

"Well, this is my style," I say looking down at my pink dress.

"Long, modest—"

"Dirty," she observes. There's a soft smile on her lips as she eyes my dress, her gaze sweeping slowly down my body to my sandalled feet. "Did you fall, Your Highness?"

Before I can answer, Hazel appears beside the other woman and says, "Your Highness, I see you've already met Lady Pénquil, the dressmaker. She has agreed to sew you as many dresses as you need for our stay."

My stomach twists.

This is the dressmaker? But she is dressed so well. Merchants don't dress like this!

The shock must show on my face because Hazel gives me a stern look. Lady Pénquil, however, looks slightly amused. Her green eyes look me up and down again, her lip curling further into a grin.

My lady-in-waiting doesn't seem to notice, she just begins talking to the dressmaker, discussing the fabrics that Lady Pénquil prefers to use when sewing and fitting dresses.

While they talk, I observe the dressmaker. She stands tall, shoulders back, head held high, like noble blood. I decide that she must be a duchess or lady who chooses to sew in her spare time. There is no other explanation.

"It would be an honour to make your dresses, Your Highness," she says, bowing slightly before me. The gesture appears genuine, aside from the smirk that still lingers in the corner of her mouth. "Tell me more about your taste in dresses, so that I may design one for you."

"We need more than one," Hazel interrupts.

"What shall you need then, Your Highness?" Lady Pénquil practically ignores Hazel as she looks closely at me, her expression somehow both sceptical and interested.

It confirms my suspicions. Only someone of noble blood would be so rude to servants.

"Several evening gowns, at least four; I can't be seen attending a ball in the same gown. A new set of undergarments," I list. "And four day-dresses, for promenading, you understand."

"Sure," the dressmaker replies simply, taking a notepad from a pocket hiding in her black and blue dress. She withdraws a pen from her hair and begins scribbling something down. "At least eight dresses. Four casual and four formals. Undergarments. Anything else?"

"A new parasol, Your Highness," Hazel suggests. "I've noticed that yours is quite tattered from the sea winds."

"Oh, yes, a parasol as well, thank you," I add.

"Brilliant," Lady Pénquil states, still scribbling quickly on her pad. "Would you please stand on the stage, here, and I'll take your measurements?"

She leads me to a sitting area on the far side of the store, where a small round stage is surrounded by comfortable chairs. I stand on the stage while she wraps a measuring tape around my waist. She writes the measurements on the back of her hand in black ink, then uses the measuring tape to take my arm and leg measurements. Soon, her hand is covered in black numbers and letters.

"How do you like your dresses?" she inquires, kneeling as she measures the inside of my calves. "I prefer a tight look, like that red dress. What do you prefer, Your Highness?"

For a moment, I picture myself wearing the dress that she is referring to. It is beautiful—but it is for too provocative! I could not wear something like that!

"I like a high neckline and a long skirt." I say it with such assertiveness that I kind of startle myself.

"Will all of your dresses appear this way?" Lady Pénquil sounds bored.

"Yes," I reply simply.

"Your Highness," Hazel cuts in, her voice low and respectful, even though she is interrupting. "Might I suggest a different style, to attract the prince's eye?"

"Which style is that?" I ask.

"Well, I noticed you admiring that red and black dress when you came in," Hazel hints, her voice nearly a whisper. "Lady Pénquil agreed that it would suit your figure quite well. The prince may also notice your figure if you wore it."

"That dress is suggestive!" I gasp. "It's not the Nashwalte way!"

"But perhaps it is the Whŷstelkiné way, and if you hope to be the queen of this land, perhaps you could consider dressing as such."

Although I can see the point my lady-in-waiting is making, that red dress is frightening. I don't like the way it makes me feel, the way the dress seems to cause a warm pool in my stomach, and tingle in my heart. The dress is dangerous!

"I think dresses like this will be just fine," I decide.

"Very well," Hazel says with a sigh.

"That style would certainly suit you, Your Highness," Lady Pénquil challenges, now standing at my side. "Not everyone can pull off a dress like that."

"I have made my choice."

"Very well."

After an hour or two at the Modiste, discussing fabrics, colours and styles, Lady Pénquil agrees to a price and promises to have the first dress ready for fitting by the evening. She says it will be rushed, but it will be a day-dress, most suited for promenading and high tea.

"You will look lovely, Your Highness," Hazel comforts as we are leaving the dressmaker's. "I'm sure Lady Pénquil will do a great job!"

"Yes, I'm sure."

"Are you all right?" Hazel checks.

My voice is short when I tell her that I am fine, just tired. My lady-in-waiting assures me that I will be able to have a rest when we get back to the East Wing of the castle, and that she will ensure that nobody disturbs me.

The afternoon comes quickly. After a nap, a spot of lunch and a quiet couple of hours reading in the castle library, Hazel collects me to walk back down to the Modiste. The sun is low in the sky when we arrive at the dressmakers for the second time today, a sunflower yellow glow reflecting off the clouds above.

"Please stand here," she says to me. Lady Pénquil holds my side with soft fingers as she steers me onto the stage. "I'll help you put on the dress, but I'll likely need to pin it for adjustments."

"How long will adjustments take?"

"Only a few minutes," she promises.

Hazel assists in unclipping my pink dress at the back, and lets the fabric slide down my back, revealing my corset and undergarments. As I step out of the dress, Hazel holds my hand to steady me, and then holds the dress while she sits in a nearby chair to wait.

The first dress the dressmaker has made me is a knee-length dress with a wide skirt. It is a pale yellow in colour, like her hair, and made of some kind of linen, with lace overlay.

When the dress is fully zipped, Lady Pénquil gathers extra

fabric at my hips, her fingers pulling the cotton tight against my skin. She pins it in several places, before she unzips the dress again and leaves me standing in my undergarments on the stage while she makes the adjustments.

Only five minutes pass, before Lady Pénquil is back with the yellow dress. She helps me into the dress and zips it up at the back. It's a snug fit, tight around my breasts and hips. There's so much fabric in the skirt that it pleats around my thighs, causing the hem to appear wavy as it hangs around my knees.

"It is beautiful!" Hazel marvels.

"It is a nice colour on you." Lady Pénquil turns the full-length mirror for me to see my reflection.

I do look lovely. Usually, I prefer darker colours that match more to my skin tone and the black of my hair. The light colour of the dress brings out the light highlights in my brown eyes and makes my silver bangles and necklace appear shinier than they are. The skirt of the dress flows outwards in a way that accentuates my natural curves, draw attention to the vastness of my hips and thick thighs, but not in a way that is overly provocative, as I had feared.

"A white cardigan and parasol would go with this dress quite nicely. Do you have those items?" the dressmaker asks.

"No," I reply. "I should like to see what that would look like."

"Of course."

Lady Pénquil brings me a parasol and cardigan, both made of the same sheer white lace, with pearly beads sewn along the edges. She slides the cardigan sleeves over my shoulders and adjusts it so that it buttons in the centre of my collar bones. As I hold the parasol in my hands, resting it upon my left shoulder, I admire myself in the mirror.

"Does it please you, Your Highness?" Lady Pénquil asks me, her voice feathery in the closeness of the room.

When I look at her, I notice that her green eyes are staring into me. It's like she's looking right through my eyes and into my brain. There's a slight quirk to her smile, one corner lifted, and a thin brown eyebrow raised just slightly. She has an expression that I would usually associate with flirtation.

"Yes," I answer simply. "It does."

Chapter 7

Now that I have a dress to wear, I am free to make my efforts with the prince. He has invited me to have a light supper with him in the garden.

The sun has set when I head out of the East Wing to meet with him, the lanterns in the garden the only light leading me to a well-manicured garden that overlooks the ocean. Stepping stones made of pavers make up a pathway lined with trimmed hedges and rose bushes. Pink and white roses bloom all through the garden, letting off a subtle floral scent.

Prince Frąviné is sitting at a small outdoor setting made of white porcelain, one leg crossed daintily over the other as he gazes into the distance. Now I notice that at the very end of the garden is a wall of grey-blue boulders that meet a line of pine trees. Past those rocks must be the cliff-face, and to the north of that would be Prince Frąviné's secret fishing place.

"Princess Aruniar," the prince says when he sees me, standing out of his seat. He gestures to the chair beside him and pulls it back from the table slightly. "Please sit."

Near the table, a lord-in-waiting stands with his hands folded in front of him. He appears to be staring across the garden, at the ocean and roaring seas.

"Don't mind him," Prince Frąviné tells me as he sits in his own chair at the same time I do. "He is here to chaperone."

"Chaperone?" I repeat. "Do we require a chaperone in your country?"

"Only if we are courting." The prince's blue eyes sparkle with flirtation, and I feel butterflies flap around in my stomach. "Do you believe us to be courting, Your Highness?"

He doesn't take his eyes off me as he sips pink liquid from a teacup, and I feel warmth gathering in my cheeks. I feel very watched as I try to make up my mind: would I prefer we were courting, or simply enjoying each other's company? That red velvet dress appears in my mind again and I feel the warmth move from my face to the pit of my stomach.

"Perhaps," I say carefully, deliberately keeping my eyes on his. "Is that what you believe us to be?"

"Well, that is a complicated question, my princess."

"How so?"

"Several women, not just in this country, but throughout many, have waited for me to ask for their hand. Why are you any different?"

"Well," I stutter awkwardly. I hadn't expected to prove my worth to the prince so soon. "I am a princess."

"I know many princesses."

"Oh."

Perhaps my day-dress is not good enough. This yellow maybe doesn't show my true beauty. Dark colours match my skin tone much more elegantly.

"Don't get me wrong, my princess, you are beautiful," he continues, as though reading my mind. "But what is different about you? Are you not just another beautiful princess, desperate to be loved and cherished by someone of royalty?"

I don't know if it is because I am tired and cranky from a long day in a strange country, or if he is right, but anger fizzles in my chest and throat as I look back at his perfect white face and square jaw. He is a snobbish twat, and I would like to tell him so.

But he is also a prince of the country that I am currently residing in, so I keep my mouth shut.

Instead, I sip my pink tea, which is now lukewarm and look off into the distance, where I can see the dark silhouette of *Sea Song* bobbing up and down with the waves of the coast.

The prince seems to notice my irritability, because he changes the subject. "How do you like the tea? Did you ask a servant what it is made from?"

"No," I reply simply. I place the teacup back on the matching saucer with a soft clink.

"I asked my lord-in-waiting," Prince Frąviné offers, his voice now soft and kind. His blue eyes are not flirtatious now, but gentle. It's strange to me how quickly his attitude has changed. "He didn't know either, but he asked the kitchen staff, and they said that red or pink rose petals are steeped in water and vanilla for a day, before they are muddled and added to boiling water to make our tea."

"That's fascinating," I reply as I take another sip, this time tasting carefully. I swish the liquid between my teeth, to get the true flavour. Perhaps I do notice a hint of vanilla. "Why do they pick red or pink, and not white? Does it change the flavour at all?"

The prince stares at me for a moment, bewilderment glazing over his features before he quickly turns to his lord-in-waiting, who is still staring over the ocean.

"Justrįkk," Prince Frąviné snaps loudly, clicking his fingers. "Justrįkk, do you know?"

"No, Your Royal Highness," the lord-in-waiting replies suddenly, still not making eye contact. "I can ask the kitchen, if you need."

"You will do anything I need," the prince growls threateningly. "Go!"

"Yes, Your Highness."

Then the lord-in-waiting is running through the rose garden and hedges. Even after he has disappeared, I can still hear his shoes tapping on the concrete and hard-wood floors throughout the castle.

"That was unnecessary," I observe.

"Yes, I know. But it was humorous, wasn't it?" The prince is still looking in the direction that the lord-in-waiting disappeared into, a nasty grin on his lips. "He is a funny one, that Justrikk."

"He's trying to please you."

"Yes, I am aware. And it is humorous to me."

This guy really is an ass hat.

His mood changes so swiftly that it seems like there is no rhyme or reason behind it; I wouldn't dare risk getting on his bad side when he holds so much power. Between the way that he treats his staff and the fact that he is rude to me, I cannot see myself entering a happy marriage with such a man.

I am about to leave the table when several servants appear with silver platters, a brilliant collection of food upon the table in front of us. My stomach makes an involuntary gurgling sound, and I suddenly realise how little I have eaten today.

On each platter is an absurd amount of food for two people. There is a platter of mixed seafood; scallops, crab and prawns; a rainbow platter of strange fruits from this land; a platter of fragrant cheeses, and a platter of exquisite sweets made of pastry and chocolate.

"What is your favourite food?" Prince Fraviné asks me when he catches me staring at the food.

"I enjoy fruit the most," I answer honestly.

"A sweet tooth." He grins. He picks up a pink fleshed slice of fruit and holds it up for me to bite. "Here. Try this fruit. It is native to our Whŷstelkiné."

"What is its name?" I ask it as I take a bite.

"Unicorn apple."

The answer catches me off guard and I spit a mouthful of the pink-fleshed fruit all over the white porcelain table. Some lands on Prince Fraviné's knee. His pants are a soft grey colour and I know instantly that the fruit will stain.

We look at each other in shock. Shame warms my neck. I feel the heat of embarrassment start to creep up my chin and into my cheeks, my heart stopping in my chest.

God Delrossa, please take me now. Spare me this humiliation.

"I am so sorry," I try nervously.

For a second, I think that the prince will yell at me, that he will treat me with the same disrespect that he treats his servants. For a moment, I wonder if he will put his hands on me.

But he laughs.

At first, it's just a smile, but then his smile cracks and he is cackling uncontrollably. He throws his head back, his hand on his stomach. Tears well in the corners of his eyes and he laughs hysterically at the tiny piece of pink fruit sinking into his pant leg.

"I can't believe you did that!" he pants between laughs, wiping his eye with one finger. "That was so funny!"

"Yeah," I chuckle awkwardly. "I guess so."

"You are certainly different from the other princesses I know, Princess Aruniar!"

I feel inclined to ask him to elaborate, but I decide that would be against my better judgement. Something tells me that I would not receive an answer that I would find flattering. So, instead of saying anything, I begin shoving food into my mouth, starting with the seafood. Perhaps the taste of the ocean will distract me from my embarrassment.

Chapter 8

Hazel is waiting for me outside my chambers when I have finished getting dressed around noon next day. Again, I am wearing the same dress as yesterday, in hopes that Lady Pénquil will have a few more dresses ready for my collection, so that I do not have to wear a dirty dress three days in a row.

When we arrive at the Modiste, the door jingles and Lady Pénquil appears suddenly from the back of the shop.

"Your Highness," she says happily when our eyes meet. "Please come in. I have two dresses ready for you. Can you try them on, and I'll make any necessary adjustments while you're here?"

"Okay," I agree.

Lady Pénquil helps me into the first dress, which is a dark shade of green. It is an evening dress made of silk. The dress is tighter than I am used to, without flowing or pleated layers; instead, the silky skirt clings to my legs on either side, making me feel the slightest bit claustrophobic.

"I don't think I like this dress," I tell her plainly, before I've had a chance to look in the mirror.

"But you look lovely," Hazel argues instantly, her voice frantic. Perhaps she is worried that I will offend the dressmaker. "That is such a nice colour on you!"

"Thank you," I sigh, unheard.

"What is the problem, Your Highness?" Lady Pénquil sounds curious, rather than offended. She's standing beside me, eyeing the dress, her hands gently jerking at the silky fabric of the skirt as she pins the fabric around my waist.

"It's too tight," I reply.

Now I am also tugging the dress. I'm trying to pull it away from my skin, but it's too snug.

What if I rip the fabric? Surely, she will be angry that I have ruined her hard work.

"Oh, that's easily fixed!"

Next thing I know, she is using a large pair of scissors to cut a line straight up the seam of the dress. She cuts a line from the hem, right to my left hip. Now there is a huge gash that runs all the way up the skirt, all frayed edges and tattered threads.

"What have you done?" I gasp.

"How does it feel now?" A wide smile is plastered on the dressmaker's face now. Her electric green eyes stare into mine, as if she is challenging me. She is still holding the giant pair of scissors. "Any better, Your Highness?"

A cold panic flushes over me. It starts at my face and ripples down my neck and chest and stomach. I feel my legs wobble with alarm as I stare at Lady Pénquil.

"You've ruined the dress!" My voice is nearly shouting. I'm in shock. I cannot believe what I've just seen.

"Not ruined," she contests. "I'd argue that I made it better. What do you think, Hazel?"

My lady-in-waiting has been watching closely from the comfy chair, not saying anything. She has an entertained smile on her face when Lady Pénquil asks her that, but I see it fade slightly when I turn to look at her.

"You look lovely, Princess," Hazel obliges.

"What, with this slit?" I argue, panic rising inside me. "Look at me! This is too provocative! It is not the Nashwalte way!"

"The prince may like it, Your Highness," Hazel tries to explain. "Remember when we discussed this? This is Whŷstelkịné. They do not have rules like ours. The dress suits you, and there is nothing wrong with getting the prince's attention. That is what you want, isn't it?"

"Not this kind of attention!"

"What kind of attention do you want?" Hazel questions. Her voice is raised. "This is the kind of attention that will get you a proposal, Your Highness. This attention will cause the prince to see you for what you are: a beautiful princess, who will bare his children. This will get you a kingdom!"

It occurs to me right now that I do not want a proposal from the prince. I do not want to marry him. He is an obnoxious man, who has no respect for his staff. Surely, he will not respect me, his suitress, if he does not respect people who perform all his tasks for him.

"You're hoping to marry Prince Frąviné?" Lady Pénquil cuts in. "Why? He is horrible."

Hazel and I both turn to look at the dressmaker. I expect that we both have a similar expression of shock on our faces, as Lady Pénquil looks from me to Hazel slowly, before her expression changes, her eyes going wide. Then, she busies herself with unzipping the dress.

"What do you mean?" Hazel asks curiously.

Lady Pénquil looks guilty. Her green eyes dart from me to my lady-in-waiting again and she clears her throat awkwardly, while she starts to remove the dress from me.

She thinks about her words carefully as she says, "I just mean... um, that royals can be... particular." The dressmaker takes the green dress to the back of the store – probably hoping to get away from this conversation – so I follow her, wearing nothing but my corset and undergarments.

"Oh, really?" I counter.

"Well, you see, Your Highness," Lady Pénquil stumbles nervously as she starts to use her sewing machine to make the adjustments she had pinned to the green silk. "Sometimes, I don't think about what I say before I say it. You shouldn't listen to me, Your Highness. I misspoke. I don't—"

"Tell me what you meant," I interrupt.

"I simply meant that sometimes the higher class, such as yourself, have very specific taste. There is nothing wrong with that."

"Of course, there isn't."

"Correct."

"So, why are you so nervous?" I press. "That can't be what you meant. So, what did you mean?"

She pulls the dress from the sewing machine and holds it up over her head to check it. She then starts to carry the dress back to the seating area around the stage, trying to get past me.

I stop her. I hold her arm firmly and look her closely in the face. There is something in her expression that I can't quite place, a word on her pink lips that goes unspoken.

"Tell me what you meant," I whisper.

"I don't know if you've noticed, Your Highness," she begins. I see now that her cheeks are turning a little red. "But his Royal Highness Prince Fraviné can be a little rude. He has very high standards, and when those standards aren't met, he can be… harsh."

"I have noticed that," I agree, talking very slowly.

"So, why would you want to marry a man like that?" Her voice is hushed, quiet in the little shop. "He is awful. I have heard many stories about him, from servants and merchants. He is not a kind prince, and he will not be a kind king. I hope to be long gone by the time that he reigns this country."

"Where will you go?"

Lady Pénquil hesitates for a second. Then she says, "I cannot answer that right now."

"I see."

"Please do not say anything, Your Highness," she pleads. "If Prince Frąviné finds out that I have spoken ill of him, there's no telling what he'll do."

"I understand. I won't say a word," I promise.

While at the Modiste, I try on two more dresses, both of which are day-dresses. Hazel carries the dresses over her arm as we walk back to the grey stone castle.

"I must speak to my father," I explain to Hazel when we reach the castle door. "We need to discuss my previous plan to marry Prince Frąviné."

"Have you changed your mind, Princess?" Hazel questions. There's concern in her voice, which makes me feel a little sick.

When I look at her, there is that familiar worry line in her forehead, her caramel eyes almost pleading when they look into mine. It squeezes my heart, knowing that I may let her and my kingdom down, but my mind is made up.

"I just need to speak to my father," I repeat.

As I walk through the castle, I look all over for King Kelriaq. I expect that he is probably drinking a mug of beer, while overlooking a pretty view. He's probably half-cut, reliving his glory days, telling stories of his days as a voyager to anyone who will listen.

After about ten minutes of looking, I find him sitting at a large table, alone, drinking beer from a mug and eating chicken off the bone. We'd brought the chickens as a gift to this country, to thank Queen Nyssra for her hospitality, and here he is, King of Nashwalte, with chicken shreds in his beard and juices running down his arms, creating tiny pools at his elbows on the wooden table. My father makes a growling sort of sound when he eats. It can be quite disturbing, especially when I was younger – but also a little embarrassing when we have company, or when we are guests at another family's castle.

"Father." I take a seat on a wooden chair beside him. Then I change my mind and move to the next seat up, in case he gets the chicken on my new dress.

"Mm," he grunts in reply through his chicken bone.

"Father, there is something I'd like to discuss with you." I keep my voice low, in fear that someone may overhear me.

"Please speak up, Aruniar," he snarls between bites and slurps of chicken. "You know that your father is getting old!"

"I'd like to talk to you about something. It's in relation to my betrothal."

At this, King Kelriaq stops. He places the chicken bone on the platter before him and wipes his mouth on a fabric napkin. The oil and chicken shreds come off his beard and hands and stain the napkin a slight yellow tint.

"He has proposed to you?" His voice is so full of hope that it breaks my heart that I must disappoint him as well.

"Not yet, Father," I sigh.

"Well, what could you possibly have to discuss with me?" King Kelriaq groans. He sounds angry. "Get back out there and attain his attention. Please, Aruniar, you are running out of time."

"That's what I want to discuss with you."

My father starts to pick up a new piece of chicken, but I gently put my hand on his wrist to stop him. I inch closer to him, so that he is looking directly into my eyes.

"Father, the prince is horrid," I say in a hushed tone. "He is rude and unkind and arrogant. He does not care about anyone but himself."

"I will not have you engaging in gossip about your future husband."

"It is not gossip. It is true. I have observed it," I explain. "Have you seen the way he speaks to his staff? Have you heard the things he has said, the way he has spoken to me? It is appalling—"

"Aruniar!" My father says my name in a way that makes me feel small. "This match has been secured for years. It is for the best of both of our countries that you and the Prince of Whŷstelkiné marry. If you care not for the interests of yourself, consider the interests of your country. Not all matches are love matches, surely you know that!"

"So, you don't care that he's obnoxious and rude? You want me to marry him anyway?"

"It is right for our country," my father insists.

"What about what is right for me?"

"Aruniar, this *is* right for you." The king's voice is strict as he frowns at me, his black eyebrows furrowing. "You are too young to understand, but this is not just about you. You are a princess. It is your responsibility to think about your people, not your own selfish needs."

Disappointment sears my heart. I thought that my father would understand. I thought that he would agree that the Prince of Whŷstelkiné is horrible and no match for his daughter.

But I was wrong. It turns out that my father only cares about his country, not his family.

Salty tears sting my eyes as I leave the table. I go straight to my chambers, where I sit at the end of the balcony that overlooks the ocean. Through blurry vision, impaired by my tears, I watch the waves below crash into the cliff. I hear the birds calling to each other as they soar through the sky. Envy cuts me deep as I watch them, my eyes leaking beads of sadness down my cheeks and neck. How I wish I was a bird, free to fly away and never see Whŷstelkiné again.

Chapter 9

It is early the next morning when Hazel knocks on the door to my chambers. I have been here since the argument with my father, not showing for dinner or an after-dinner drink the prince had invited me to. When someone knocked at the door late last night, I had pretended to be asleep.

The birdsong outside my window reminds me of home as I sit up in bed. The covers are cold and soft beneath my skin, the fuzzy blanket of fur slipping down my legs just as my lady-in-waiting enters the room.

"Good morning, Your Highness." Hazel smiles as she closes the door behind her. "I was coming to deliver a message from His Royal Highness Prince Fraviné."

"Can't it wait?" I sigh, turning away from her to rub the sleep from my eyes. "It's far too early for that self-centred prick."

"That is no way to speak of someone you are destined to marry."

Hearing that makes me more annoyed. She is right, but I don't like it. If I were able to run away, like Lady Pénquil, I would. I would take all my things and disappear into the night... but I can't. It is my duty to take care of my country... and besides, someone would recognise me and drag me back to my father. In this country of beige elves, I am as noticeable as a red poppy among the grass.

"Here." Hazel holds out a silver tray with a small envelope on top. "This may raise your spirits, Your Highness."

Reluctantly, I take the envelope from the tray, my fingernails grazing the silver and making a soft scraping sound as I do so. The wax seal on the envelope is a shade of blue, shimmering in the morning sun. It doesn't surprise me that the house seal resembles the sea beast, long and twisted like a serpent, belly disappearing among the waves, is the very same as the one featured on the Whŷstelkiné flag.

With quick fingers, that have had a lot of practise opening sealed envelopes, I rip open the top and withdraw a hand-size piece of parchment.

"What is it, Your Highness?" Hazel asks, although the expression on her face tells me that she already knows.

"It is an invitation to a ball," I answer. "Tonight. That's kind of late notice."

"Good thing you have a dress, Your Highness," my maid observes.

The morning goes quickly. After a shower and dressing, I have a light breakfast with the prince in the garden, where we discuss the events of tonight's ball. He wants many dances, a dozen platters of seafood and pink fruit.

"You have inspired me, my princess," he charms, his eyes glinting like stars in the mid-morning sunlight.

We are drinking pink tea with pastries and colourful fresh fruits. Some of the fruit I recognise as being tropical fruits found on other islands I have visited, but what predominantly takes up the platter is the thorny pink, apparently known as the unicorn apple. Scattered over the platter, between the fruits and pastries, are some white rose petals, directly from the garden.

"How so?" I am holding a small, sweet pastry, covered in powdered white sugar between two sticky fingers.

"Usually, I'd host a small ball, and only invite the upper class," the prince explains between bites of a slice of yellow tropical fruit. The fruit drips sugary sweetness onto the porcelain table and into the prince's lap. "But since you told me that you also invite peasants to your balls, I've been thinking that perhaps it could be quite fun to see more people from Whŷstelkiné dressed up."

His words surprise me. I had thought him a superficial classist with only a care for riches and women's attention. Perhaps I have had an impact on him. If that is the case, maybe I could change him, inspire him to be a better king.

"I see."

"Perhaps there are more beautiful women in this kingdom than I know," he goes on. "The more beautiful women, the better."

Maybe not.

"I want lots of dancing at this ball," Prince Frąviné continues, now using a napkin to wipe some of the fruit juice off his pants. "I would like to see my options."

Of course, you would, I nearly say.

"Do you dance at balls, my princess?" he asks me.

"I do."

"Which dances do you like? I shall have to organise the music to your taste," he says, a crooked smile on his thin, pink lips. "As long as your taste complements mine."

"I enjoy a waltz," I answer simply, ignoring his obvious jab.

"A waltz. Don't you think that could leave our guests feeling a tad bored? How about a foxtrot?"

"A foxtrot is fine, but a waltz is lovely. It will give you time to chat with each guest, which is what you desire, isn't it?" I enquire.

"Yes, but what do you desire?"

His gaze is intense now, his blue eyes stifling as they stare into mine, less like looking and more like examining. It feels almost uncomfortable.

"How about a tango?" I suggest.

"A tango!" the prince sounds aghast. He shakes his head in disbelief, as though I have made a ridiculous suggestion. "That's not happening."

"Why not? Don't you know how to tango?"

"Of course, I do!"

"Then what's the problem?" I challenge.

"It's not very elegant, is it?" he says thoughtfully, stroking his chin. "Not like a foxtrot."

"How is a foxtrot more elegant than a tango?"

"Trust me, Princess." He chuckles. "I know what I'm saying."

"Fine, we'll have a waltz and one foxtrot," I compromise, putting down the last of my sugary pastry. "No tango."

"That doesn't seem like much dancing."

"Two waltzes then."

"Two waltzes and a foxtrot, no tango," the prince agrees.

"Perfect."

The prince tells me of his plan to host more balls if this one goes well. He explains that he would like them to be themed, but as this is the first he will be hosting with me as his special guest, he wants the first one to be quite basic.

"I wouldn't want to scare you off with an exotic theme," he teases. "I know that women as fragile as you scare easy."

What a pig.

"How am I fragile?" I snap back. "There is nothing fragile about me!"

Prince Fr̦aviné snorts with amusement. He shakes his head, chuckling to himself. And then he reaches out a hand and pushes my black curls back behind my right ear, looking at me tenderly.

"You really are very different from the other women I have courted, my princess," he tells me.

"Is that a bad thing?" I clarify.

"It depends on who you ask."

The setting sun reflects a bright orange glow on the sea when Hazel helps me into my new green dress that evening. The air is cool on my bare shoulders as the salty wind rushes over the waves, the slightest amount of ocean spray touching my face as I stand on the balcony.

The green silk feels tight on my skin, especially around my wide hips and bust. The fabric is soft and cold along my stomach and catches just the smallest amount of sunset light from the ocean.

A small vibrating sound emanates from the zip at the back of the dress, as Hazel finishes assisting me with dressing.

"How would you like your hair this evening, Your Highness?" Hazel asks me.

"I want traditional Nashwaltian braids, to show my pride for my country," I answer, looking down at the green hem around my thighs. Even with the slit in the side, the hem is tight on my skin. "But with fresh roses from the garden."

"White roses?"

"Yes, thank you."

"Perhaps some baby's breath, too," Hazel suggests.

"Whatever you think."

"I shall not be long," Hazel tells me, as she heads out of the chambers.

I wait on the balcony, leaning my body weight on my hands, looking out at the sea.

The diving birds are soaring over the water, calling to each other and plummeting head-first into the crashing waves. They reappear, bursting from the water, with a fish in their beak, before they flap their wings and disappear.

The sound of the ocean calms me. The wind over the sea and the waves crashing into the cliff is a relaxing combination. Even with the anxiety of being in a new place, surrounded by elves that I do not know, where I am out of place and alone, one thing remains the same: the sound of crashing waves, constant and serene.

"I've returned," Hazel announces as she closes the heavy wooden door behind her.

I stay leaned over the balcony as she braids my hair. Her fingers are quick at twisting and turning my dark curls, winding and weaving flower stems between them until my hair looks like a royal garden. When she shows me my reflection in a small hand-held mirror, I feel a puddle of homesickness in my stomach.

The person in the reflection looks so much like my mother that the image cuts a pang of grief into my chest. I cannot look away.

"What's wrong, Your Highness?" Hazel asks suddenly. "Do you not like it? It's no different than what I usually do."

"I like it," I mumble. "Thank you, Hazel."

"Are you nervous about tonight?" Hazel nods her head. "I understand. It is a very important ball. The prince will see you receive his people for the first time. But there is no need to be nervous; you are beautiful, and the prince is certain to notice."

"You are right," I agree, admiring my likeness to my mother in my reflection. Something like pride comes over me. "I do look beautiful."

Chapter 10

The music from below can heard throughout the kingdom. There are several musicians, and an orchestra in the ballroom downstairs. They arrived at the castle, a while ago, pushing wooden carts that held all their instruments and equipment. Hazel and I had watched them from the balcony, as she helped me prepare for the ball.

"Shall we meet the prince now, Your Highness?" Hazel offers, now that I am all dolled up. "I'm sure he is waiting for you downstairs."

"Yes," I agree. "We should meet him now."

With one last look in the mirror, and a quick spritz of my vanilla and jasmine scented perfume, Hazel and I leave my chambers. We head down the staircase, my silver shoes clicking lightly on the grey stone steps. I hold the railing with one hand, my long fingernails glimmering in the warm yellow light from the chandeliers.

"I shall leave you here," Hazel whispers to me when we reach the bottom of the stairs. "Go and meet your prince. Have a wonderful night."

"What will you do?"

"I will be here, should you need me," Hazel assures me.

From here, I can hear the hum of conversation vibrating through the echoey corridors of the castle. In the empty rooms, rich with space and high ceilings, the sounds of a lively party drift through the walls and into my ears.

As I enter the ballroom, I am surprised to see how many decorative pieces the prince has organised for the ball. There are massive bouquets of white roses in tall, silver vases placed on tables with white tablecloths, the room glinting with diamonds. There are even bunches of white roses hanging from the chandeliers. There's a table nearby holding a tower of bubbling yellow champagne. I grab a glass as I walk by.

Many people, most of them fair-skinned with golden hair, are gathered in the ballroom. A sea of elegant dresses, made of tulle and delicate fabrics, swarm the huge room, jewellery and riches glinting in the light from the crystal chandeliers overhead.

I look out at the crowd of well-dressed citizens, searching for a familiar face. There, near the entrance to the castle, stands the prince, holding a glass of champagne and wearing a white tuxedo, a glittering gold tie around his neck that perfectly matches his crown. We make eye contact.

"Princess Aruniar," Prince Frąviné says loudly as he comes over to me. He tips up his glass and finishes the last of his drink.

How many has he had?

"Hello," I reply casually.

"Come and meet the duke," Prince Frąviné slurs. Obviously, that is not his first glass of champagne. "He is lovely. My childhood friend."

Before I have time to answer, he's grasped a large, white hand around my elbow. He leads me through a sea of guests towards the door of the castle, where another young man is standing, his suit white with gold trim, like a fairytale prince. He's chatting to a group of young ladies, all of whom are dressed in delicate dresses, laughing and touching the women on their shoulder or hip while they speak.

The women seem to disperse as we approach. One lady,

taller than me and thin like a spaghetti noodle, casts a glare that shudders me to my core.

"Duke Lindîn!" Prince Frąviné shouts as we approach.

"Frąviné, my old friend!" the duke replies, clapping the prince on the shoulder in a friendly manner. "It feels like years since we last met!"

"You simply must meet my date for the evening." Prince Frąviné drags me forward a few steps, his grip tight on my wrist. "She is a princess."

"A princess," Duke Lindîn greets, extending a hand for me to take. He kisses my hand, but he isn't looking at my eyes, rather the pearl necklace around my collarbone, and then his eyes drift a bit lower. "Lovely to meet you."

"Likewise," I reply shortly, though it feels untrue.

"And does the princess have a name?" the duke questions, his wicked green eyes still mulling over my body.

His eyes are hooded, his expression is unreadable as he looks at me through his lashes. It makes my stomach curl uncomfortably, and I take a small step back from him, withdrawing my hand from his.

"Princess Aruniar of Nashwalte," I tell him.

The duke looks offended that I have moved away from him, but he doesn't say so. He just keeps watching me with those piercing eyes, focussing on my bust and other curves of my body. I'd like to punch his nose.

Are all men in this kingdom complete idiots?

"Can I get you something to drink, Your Highness?" Duke Lindìn offers.

"She is my date, Lindìn." The prince steps between us, as though he is shielding me. Then he adds in a hushed tone, "And I do not like the way you are looking at her."

"But she is beautiful," Duke Lindìn purrs.

"Don't make me hurt you."

"You really are so sensitive, Frąviné," the duke snorts, giving the prince a gentle shove on his shoulder. "I'm only joking. When have I ever taken something of yours?"

Is this how men speak about women when women are not around? Why are they doing it in front of me? Is it because they are both drunk that they think I do not notice their objectifying comments? Or are they just being obnoxious? The men back home do not speak of women this way, and if they do, they at least have the decency to do it in private.

"Not taken," the prince agrees. "But you have borrowed something of mine many times."

"*Borrowed* being the key word!"

"You shall not borrow what is mine tonight, Lindìn, I guarantee that!"

"Luckily," I interject boldly, "I do not belong to you, Prince Frąviné. Or anyone else for that matter." I look from one man to the other. "The way you speak of women is inexcusable, and I shall have nothing to do with either of you for the rest of the night!"

The group of women nearby stop their conversation. Over their champagne glasses, they watch me storm away, my heels clicking dramatically on the wooden floor. I feel their eyes on me, staring into my back. I hear whispering but I am too angry to be embarrassed.

Leaving the ballroom and castle all together, I race down the grey steps. When I've reached halfway and believe that I am far enough away from them, I plop down on a stone stair, my knees curled up in front of me.

What an arrogant prick! Both of them! What would my

father say if he heard the Prince of Whŷstelkiné talking about me like that?

I hang my head, hiding my face in my hands. I take deep breaths to try to steady my heartbeat.

"Leaving the party so soon?" I hear a familiar voice.

When I look up, I am shocked to see the velvet red dress standing before me. The dress is shorter than my green silky one, strapless, the black trim running along the bottom hem of the skirt and outlining details of the dress, including the side seams and love-heart neckline. It is more beautiful than I remember.

Then I see the dressmaker's face. She is smiling a sort of lop-sided smile, her eyes twinkling, as she looks down at me. Her hair is not pinned back tonight, but twisted into perfect, yellow waves around her face, stopping at her elbows.

"Just taking a break," I tell her firmly, though my breath betrays me.

Lady Pénquil sits down on the step beside me. She's wearing a pair of shiny black shoes that match her black and red velvet dress surprisingly well. For the first time since I've met her, her lips are outlined in dark red lipstick and a small amount of charcoal rests on her eyelids. The darkness really brings out the colour of her eyes, and I find myself staring.

"You look nice," I compliment.

"Thank you." The smile on her red lips grows much wider now. "I made this dress myself. I love your dress as well, by the way. Who is your modiste?"

"Very funny." I roll my eyes.

There is silence between us for a moment. Perhaps, I have offended her.

"I have never been to a ball," Lady Pénquil says, looking up the stairs, her green eyes glimmering with excitement. "Will there be dancing?"

"There will be much dancing. Perhaps too much."

I cringe at the thought of having to dance with either of those two disgusting men and consider staying out here for the remainder of the ball.

"Well, I would like to dance," Lady Pénquil states. "Perhaps you will join me."

"Perhaps not."

"You can be very grouchy, can't you?" Although her words are rude, she says it in a tone that sounds like a joke. "What has you sitting out here by yourself anyway?"

"My date is revolting."

"I could have told you that!" Lady Pénquil laughs.

"And the duke is no better," I sigh, putting my head back in my hands. "I might have thought that there was one decent man on this island."

"There are decent men here," she assures me. "You just haven't met them yet."

I stop myself from arguing any further, deciding that there is no point. Of course, she believes that there are decent men here; this is her home.

"I do not have a date tonight."

"Yes, I see that."

"Come with me, Your Highness. I will accompany you," she offers, extending her hand for me to take.

"Is that allowed?"

I take her hand. Something about it makes my stomach twist, but she pulls me to my feet, and the feeling is gone.

She is stronger than she looks.

"Women accompany each other all the time," Lady Pénquil says with a shrug of her shoulders, releasing my hand. "Perhaps you can tell me about your country while we dance. I love to hear about faraway lands."

It occurs to me that in the few days that I have been here, no one, not even the prince, has asked me about my homeland. No one has asked about my country, my family, my traditions. Lady Pénquil is the first to show an interest.

"That would be nice."

As we walk up the steps together, the dressmaker asks me about my home. She wants to know what my castle looks like, how my country looks compared to Whŷstelkiné. She asks what Nashwalte's traditions are, and I am more than pleased to answer.

"The Day of Life is a celebration of our Goddess, Frewope the Devoted," I explain as we stand together in a quiet corner of the ballroom, a glass of champagne in hand.

"That sounds fascinating." Lady Pénquil's expression is genuine. Her emerald eyes gaze into mine with a fondness that I can't quite place. "What do you do on this day?"

"The day begins at sunrise. The whole kingdom joins to thank Frewope the Devoted and praise her for her generosity of food and water over the year. Then, we plant trees in town, and eat the fruits. All who live in the kingdom join to have meals in the square and give thanks on this day."

"That sounds lovely."

"It is."

Lady Pénquil has more questions. She wants to know whether our laws are different and what kind of flowers grow in the gardens. She asks about the Royal Family, and the history of our people. She wants to know about wars and rebellions, allies and enemies. She has many questions, and I spend hours answering them as we drink champagne together.

When the first waltz begins, I am hesitant to join, but Lady

Pénquil insists that she will be my first partner. We start off dancing together. She takes the lead, as I do not know how to lead a waltz.

On my waist, I can feel her cold hand through my silk dress. My skin tingles where our bodies meet, sending a soft shiver down my spine, warming my cheeks and the well of my stomach. Her fingers entwine with mine as we dance. Her hands are soft. Her hands are cold. Her eyes are locked on mine. It's almost intoxicating, the way she gazes into my eyes.

In the flurry of it all, I accidentally step on her feet a couple of times.

"Sorry!" I gasp.

But she doesn't mind. Apparently, Lady Pénquil has had her feet stepped on before, because her red smile doesn't even falter when she says, "That happens all the time!"

"I thought you'd never been to a ball before?" I recall.

"I haven't." She shrugs, letting my waist go so that I can spin to the music. When we are facing each other again, she adds, "Just because I haven't been to a royal ball doesn't mean I've never danced before."

"Do you attend many parties?"

"All the time. People throw parties all over town!" She's smiling broadly, as though she finds my curiosity amusing.

That's when we swap partners. Lady Pénquil releases my hand and I spin to my next partner. This partner is a man I have not met. He has a round face that appears slightly younger than me, and his gold hair is astonishingly frizzy.

"You must be Princess Aruniar of Nashwalte," the young man says to me with a genuine smile. He has perfectly straight, white teeth. "It is lovely to meet you."

"And who might you be?" I ask.

"Lord Jorhwûrn," he introduces politely. "I have heard many things about you from Prince Fṛaviné. He and I have known each other for quite some time. He thinks very highly of you."

"And why shouldn't he?" I challenge.

"He is correct in thinking so much of you, Your Highness," Lord Jorhwûrn flatters as he lets me spin. "You are very beautiful."

"Thank you."

I spin away from him to meet my new dance partner, another young man with long blond hair tied back in a loose ponytail at the back of his head. This man has quite a sturdy jaw, almost like a square. He has a raised scar on his chin, jagged and long, almost like a lightning bolt.

"An honour to meet you, Your Highness," he says to me in a quiet tone. "You are looking lovely tonight. That dress… it is dangerous, no?"

The mention of my dress shocks me. I had forgotten all about the dress I am wearing. I had forgotten to be nervous about looking too unchaste. I had felt beautiful. I had felt liberated. But now I am feeling scared and uneasy. There is a sick feeling urging in my stomach when I look in this square-jawed man's eyes, how he looks me up and down, like I am something to be stared at.

Looking across the dance floor at Lady Pénquil, I wonder whether men are asking her inappropriate questions as well.

"Did I offend you, Your Highness?" the man asks me. "I only meant that you look so beautiful that I would like to see you without the dress."

My body feels numb with panic.

I push this square-faced man away from me, stepping back from him. I cannot believe what he has said to me.

"It is a compliment, Your Highness!" he defends, now

looking around to see if anyone is looking at us. He reaches out to take my hand again.

Fear stirs in my stomach like a cauldron. I think I am about to be sick. My head swims with terror. This time, without thinking, I raise my hand to defend myself against him, as he takes another step closer to me.

I hear a *thwack*.

Next thing I know, the square-faced man is holding his cheek. There are tears in his eyes as he stares at me in shock.

The entire ballroom is quiet. Even the music has stopped.

Everyone is staring at us.

Hundreds of eyes wait eagerly for the next event.

I am frozen.

The man staggers slightly as he looks at his hand, presumably to see if his face is bleeding. It isn't, but there's a red mark in the shape of a handprint plastered across his cheek.

"That is not how you speak to a lady," is all I can muster. My breath escapes me, and my voice comes out quiet, but no less outraged. "Let that be a lesson to you."

Without another word, the square-faced man turns on his heel and storms out of the ballroom. He keeps his head down, lightly touching his slapped cheek as he leaves. I hope that he is embarrassed. His shoes click on the grey steps outside, and there is silence in the ballroom for another few seconds before Prince Fraviné is at my side.

"Go about your business." He chuckles. "Nothing to see here."

He grips my forearm in his large, firm hand, and I nearly slap him as well—but I stop myself. The prince leads me off the dance floor, into a quiet corner. The chatter in the ballroom starts up again when we are out of sight.

"What happened?" he whispers to me.

"He offended me!"

"Lord Kortràä is a good man. What could he have done to offend you?"

"He made comments about seeing my body naked," I tell him in a whisper.

The prince blinks at me. He is quiet for a second, apparently thinking about this. Then he says, "And this offends you?"

"Of course, it does!"

"He called you beautiful," Prince Frąviné tries to defend. "How can you not see that he was complimenting you?"

"That is not how I wish to be complimented," I reply, folding my arms over my chest. "It is rude and unnecessary."

"Lord Kortràä is my friend," the Prince of Whŷstelkiné sneers threateningly. His face is very close to mine, and I can smell the alcohol on his breath. "Perhaps you have forgotten that you are a visitor to my country, and I can have you thrown out for embarrassing me at my own ball!"

"You do not scare me, Prince Frąviné," I hiss at him. "I will not be threatened."

"And I will not have ungrateful guests."

He turns away from me and goes back to the dance floor, where the orchestra has started to play again. It's playing an upbeat tune, and most guests are doing the foxtrot.

Lady Pénquil is not. She is leaning against a stone wall, holding two glasses of champagne in her hands. She holds one out to me when I approach her.

"That was interesting," she smirks impishly.

"Hardly." I drink the whole glass of champagne in about five seconds flat and then place the empty flute on the nearest surface.

"You don't need to drink that fast, Your Highness." Lady Pénquil smiles. "You realise that the ball still has quite a few hours left. The champagne will not go to waste, I assure you."

I ignore her.

As a servant passes me with a silver tray of champagne flutes, I snatch two. I down one quickly and hold the other in my hand. Already, I am starting to sway, my legs feeling a little like tall trees in the wind.

"Whoa." Lady Pénquil steadies me by holding my side with her fingertips. "Maybe I should take this off you."

"If you take this glass," I tell her slowly, "I will have you executed."

The dressmaker smiles widely at my threat, as though it is a joke, but I do not see what is funny. I continue to sip my champagne, fully aware of the cold hands that hold my hips in place.

Just then, Prince Frąviné's voice is loud and demanding through the ballroom. The music quietens as he is calling everyone to attention.

"That concludes our ball," he shouts to the crowd of people. "Thank you for attending. I shall host another ball soon."

And with that, all the guests begin to leave. There is the clinking sound of glasses being placed on tables and silver trays as people shuffle out of the ballroom. Lady Pénquil leaves with them.

Within a couple of minutes, it's just the prince and I standing alone in the ballroom.

"Apart from your outburst, that was a nice evening," Prince Frąviné tells me. "I shall host another ball tomorrow, I think."

"Tomorrow?" I repeat. "Don't you think that's a bit soon?"

"Not at all," the prince replies. "I'm going to need to host many balls to see whether you are always this careless with my guests. Because if you are, there are plenty of eligible women in this country who would like to marry me."

Then he walks away from me.

Chapter 11

During a quiet breakfast with my father in the morning, he mentions that he heard about my argument with the prince. At first, I think that I should be embarrassed, but something else ticks into my chest. Pride, perhaps.

"Yes, because he is a prick," I hiss, keeping my voice low. "He expects me to allow shallow and disgusting men to sexualise me. I was insulted."

"Princess Aruniar," my father sighs, also speaking quietly. "You need the prince to marry you."

"I do not want to marry him."

"He may change," the king tells me firmly. "With your advice and support, he may become a very noble king."

"I don't have time to change a man!" I snap at my father. For a second, I forget to whisper.

"Things take time," King Kelriaq tells me patiently. "You have to be patient with men. And you do have time. You have your whole life."

I groan into my breakfast.

"Apologise to him," my father tells me. "An apology could go a long way."

"I have nothing to apologise for!" I whisper-shout.

"Aruniar!" The king takes a deep breath. For the first time, he puts down his toast and looks at me. "Marriages take compromise."

"Father—"

"Sometimes, compromise means apologising, even when you did nothing wrong. Your mother, Delrossa rest her soul, knew that long before I did. She taught me some very important things about marriage."

"But I don't want a marriage with him, Father."

"What you want does not outweigh the needs of your country," King Kelriaq replies simply.

Just then, Prince Fṛaviné comes to me at the dining table, and my father goes back to eating his breakfast. The prince sits beside me, sipping a cup of pink tea. His hair is slicked back, tied in a loose bun at the back of his head, his green eyes glimmering in the morning sunlight.

"Good morning, my princess," he says in a soft voice. "How did you sleep?"

"Quite well," I answer, coolly.

I'm surprised that he is in such high spirits after our disagreement the night before. He seems almost cheerful.

"So did I."

"I was quite exhausted from the dancing at that ball you hosted. It was a lovely night."

"I agree." He nods.

We are quiet for a moment, and my father clears his throat in between bites of toast. I nearly roll my eyes, but I catch myself, because the prince is staring at me. Instead, I inch closer to him and feign a warm smile, the way a princess is taught to smile.

"Would you like to go for a walk?" I ask.

"I'd be honoured to walk with you," Prince Fṛaviné replies happily. "There is a lovely private beach I can show you. Come with me."

I follow him into the garden. Through the rose gardens and

hedges, the prince leads me past the side of the castle and into the trees. From the top of the cliff, I can see a narrow pathway that leads down a slightly less steep space in the rock-face.

"That looks a bit steep," I tell Prince Frąviné nervously.

"I've got you," he promises.

The prince holds my hand as we step slowly down the side of the cliff. He leads me into the bushy forest. It is a minute's walk to a small cove that I assume is the private beach he invited me to.

"I would like to apologise for how I acted last night," I begin. "It was inappropriate to speak to you the way I did."

"I understand," the prince replies. "I have been informed that your country has a different way of doing things. Our countries are dissimilar."

"That is correct."

"It will take time for you to adapt to Whŷstelkiné," the prince continues. "I cannot expect you to understand everything overnight."

"Right, and I can't expect you to understand everything I do either."

"I do not need to understand." The prince shrugs. "You will be living here, and I will never leave my country. Why should I need to learn your ways?"

"Maybe because you respect me and my home?"

Prince Frąviné seems to consider this. His face looks puzzled, but he is quiet for a moment, and I hope that perhaps something I have said has made him think. He isn't quite looking at me; more like he is looking past me, over my left shoulder at the water. His slender hands fiddle with the small seashells he wears as jewellery around his wrist.

"I have decided to host another ball," he says suddenly.

"Oh?"

It catches me by surprise, perhaps because it's so unrelated to what I had been talking about. It seems like an unnatural pivot in conversation, and I wonder whether he has thought at all about my perspective.

"Tonight. And I would like a theme," Prince Frąviné elaborates.

"A theme?"

"A masquerade! Isn't it a great idea? One of the women from the ball last night suggested it," he rambles, grinning widely. "I'm very excited about it."

"I bet."

We spend another few minutes exploring the private beach. The prince says that this beach below the castle is called Syppŷreqkïn Beach. It is named so, because few Whŷstelkiné citizens know of its existence. It is a royal secret. According to Prince Frąviné, it is the most beautiful beach on the island.

"Are there many beaches here?" I question as I stand in a shallow rock pool, where tiny, friendly hermit crabs crawl around my bare beet.

"No others are safe for swimming," the prince explains. "You would not swim in sea beast waters, would you?"

"Of course not."

"Only some of the coastline is used for fishing and docking."

Fishing does not interest me. "And what of this sea beast?"

"Eéijrwărpmąs. It is a monster."

"What kind of monster?"

Prince Frąviné thinks for a moment. He seems to stare off into the distance, looking over the ocean, tapping his forefinger on his lip as he does so. I can see that in the short time we have been out here in the sun, his cheeks have already started to pinken with the hot kiss of sunshine.

"Oh, it is enormous. A dragon below the water," the prince tells me, his description sounding rather ambiguous. "The size of the castle, at least."

"Has anyone ever seen it?"

"The tale of Eéijrwărpmąs is not a legend!" There's an offended tone to his voice, as though I have wounded him. "He is a mighty beast, powerful enough to sink a hundred ships!"

"I see," is all I say in reply. "What are his powers?"

"He controls the tides," the prince answers, a casual tone returning to his voice and his words as he turns back to the water. "He controls the waves. A single splash of his tail is enough to cause tidal waves. He creates storms and cyclones that have destroyed cities."

"Sounds dangerous," I observe.

"He most certainly is."

"Have *you* ever seen it?"

"Never. Though, I have the sense to fear him. Only those who doubt his magnificent power fall prey to his perils."

"Is this the creature I've seen on your island's flag?" I ask.

"The very same," the prince nods.

Intriguing.

"Does this information scare you, my princess?" Prince Frąviné asks me.

"It definitely interests me."

"Are you often fascinated by things that could be lethal?"

"Only when I don't believe in them," I reply simply.

At this, the prince looks offended. His gold eyebrows furrow and he makes a thoughtful humming sound, before he starts walking back towards the castle, apparently deciding that our trip to the private beach is over.

That evening, the music starts quite early. There is already dancing before many guests have arrived. I do not see Lady Pénquil on the crowded dance floor, and I wait nervously by the entrance for her. Some guests greet me, more women than men – probably due to my assault on Lord Kortràä last night – but not as many I had imagined. Some whisper as they walk by me, some look me up and down. I know they are gossiping about me, but I pay it no mind. I will not have men making sexual comments about my body.

I stand by the door for quite some time, greeting guests and drinking from my champagne flute. I cannot see Lady Pénquil anywhere.

All the guests are masked. Even I am masked – but my hair and skin tone are an obvious giveaway to who I am, unlike many of the citizens of Whŷstelkiné; many of them have similar physical traits.

"Might you fancy a dance?" a familiar voice asks me.

When I turn to see who is speaking to me, I am shocked to learn that it is not the person I associate with that voice, but rather a young man in a black tuxedo. He has long blond hair tied back in a loose braid and freckles upon his cheeks. His eyes are emerald, green, under his black sequined mask.

"I might," I reply.

The man extends his hand to me, and I take it gratefully. His hands are cold on mine as he leads me to the dance floor, where the music is playing a soft and gentle tune. As he places one hand on my hip, he moves slowly and gracefully to the music. I follow.

We lock eyes as we sway, my fingers touching his shoulder and my face close to his. This man is tender, and he dances so smoothly. He holds one arm up high over my head and I twirl under it for a moment, before I catch a whiff of his scent. It is familiar. It is floral, lavender.

"What is your name?" I ask the masked man.

A wry smile appears on the masked man's lips, curling up much further on one side than the other. Although most of his face is masked, I am sure that I recognise him.

"Lord Pénquil."

Recognition flashes across my face and I stare at them for a long moment.

Lord Pénquil. Lady Pénquil.

"But you are wearing a suit," I gasp.

"I am, aren't I?"

"Is that allowed?"

"Well, I don't see why not!" Lady Pénquil sounds amused. "I made it, after all. Why shouldn't I wear my own design?"

"The design is not the issue," I whisper.

"There is no issue," she argues plainly. "I wear what I like, and so should you."

"I need a drink," I tell her.

As I walk away from Lady Pénquil, I notice that the prince is standing on the outside of the dancefloor. His arms are crossed, and he is watching me with close eyes. It is as though he is an eagle, and I am a mouse.

I take a flute of champagne from a passing tray and tip the drink up, so that I have downed half the flute in one mouthful. Then I take a pastry off another passing tray.

The dress I am wearing tonight is much longer than the one I wore yesterday. It is much more my usual style, violet in colour with a skirt that pleats and gathers on the floor around my feet. It is tight from the neckline to my hips, and then, with the help of a petticoat, splays outwards. It accentuates some of my

Nashwaltian curves, and hides others. It is a flattering style. My mask is the same colour as my dress, with a gold pattern across it.

"You are looking lovely." It is the same young man from yesterday with a round face and long hair. Lord Jorhwûrn. "That colour suits you."

"Thank you, My Lord," I reply. "I quite like that colour on you, too."

He is wearing a grey suit with a black tie and a black mask. It is nothing extravagant, but a classic look is a nice one.

"Thanks." He grins, sipping his champagne. "Can I interest you in a dance tonight?"

"Perhaps one."

We dance a single foxtrot, and then I am back at the corner of the room, drinking more champagne and watching masked guests spinning on the dance floor, most of them middle- and lower-class citizens.

I find myself envying them.

They do not have a king for a father, who is adamant I marry a superficial and self-important prince, who objectifies women. They are lucky. They do not have an entire country that depends on them, trusts them, and relies on them to make the right choice.

"Enjoying yourself?" Lady Pénquil asks me when she approaches, still dressed like a man.

"I suppose."

"What is wrong?" she inquires. "You seem tense."

"I am surprised to see a woman in a suit," I tell her stubbornly.

"Do you like it?"

"I have never seen it before."

"That is not what I asked."

Despite myself, I think I do like it. I like the way that the suit kind of ruffles around her breasts, the way the middle button on the suit synchs her waist. I like the way that she can dress so masculine and still be a woman. It is appealing to me.

"I think I do," I decide.

"Great." Lady Pénquil smiles, her mask shuffling the smallest amount over her cheeks. "I'm glad."

We sip more champagne. I drink fast, but she drinks slow. By the time the servants are bringing our dessert, I am onto my fifth glass of champagne, and my legs are quivering. I've spilled the slightest bit of alcohol on my dress, and now the purple silk on my left breast is slightly damp.

"It's not noticeable," Lady Pénquil had promised me when I tried to dap it with a napkin.

Suddenly, in a moment of clarity, I wonder how long Lady Pénquil has been holding my side with one hand to keep me from falling. But I don't dislike it, so I don't mention it. I also don't mention the fact that her thumb is kind of tracing my hip, a soft sensation that causes my stomach and chest to flutter excitedly. Strange, but not repulsive. In fact, it makes me curious.

When I stumble during my sixth drink, Lady Pénquil catches me, both cold hands on my waist and her face close to mine. I look into her green eyes, and I feel a tickle in the lower end of my stomach. I have never felt this sensation for a woman before. What does it mean?

Chapter 12

Lady Pénquil's eyes are locked on me. She seems to watch me the way a cat watches a mouse – but it doesn't bother me. In fact, I kind of like it.

"Do you want to get out of here?" she whispers to me, her hands still firmly holding my waist. "It's a bit crowded in here, don't you think?"

"Yes," I agree. "We should go for a walk."

"Let's."

Lady Pénquil releases my hips as I finish my final glass of champagne, feeling a little woozy. I let her take my hand and lead me out of the castle. As we go down the steps, the only light to guide us the dim yellow lamps overhead.

"Where are we going?" I ask, my voice sounding a little slurred.

"You'll see."

I follow her down the street and into a dark alleyway. In the darkness, I stumble over a loose rock on the sandy road, but she catches me, using her weight to hold mine. When we are standing together in the alley, Lady Pénquil leans against a grey wall, and I do the same to the opposite wall, facing her. By the light of the moon, I can just make out Lady Pénquil's smile, under the black mask.

"What are we doing out here?" I ask her, my brain feeling a little bit fuzzy as the alcohol begins to hit me.

"It's not crowded out here, is it?"

"No."

"Do you think this is better?" Lady Pénquil's voice is light. She is smiling at me, and her head is cocked to the side, as though she is a curious bird.

"Definitely."

When we are silent for a moment, I take the time to look up at the starry night sky.

Before I know it, Lady Pénquil has moved so that she is standing beside me, leaning against the stone wall, her left shoulder slightly touching my right shoulder. There's an electric buzzing in my skin where hers has touched. It ignites something inside me, sets my heart aflame. I feel it racing in my chest. I feel something singe my ribs and throat. It hurts, but in a good way. I never want it to end.

When I turn to look at her, her face is a centimetre from mine. Her green eyes sparkle. What is this strange feeling flooding my system? What is this warmth? This tickle? It's deep in my stomach, it aches in my body. It feels wonderful and horrible at the same time and it's all because of...

"You look beautiful," Lady Pénquil whispers to me.

"Thank you," I mumble, sudden shyness making my cheeks redden. "You look... handsome."

Lady Pénquil looks down at her clothes and does a funny kind of twirl, from side to side as she admires her own handy work. At first, it was a confused look that touched her face, but now a smile creeps onto her lips and when our eyes meet again, she is intense.

"You really like it?" There's a worry to her voice that kind of makes my heart squeeze, and I wonder how many other people in this town know that Lady Pénquil sometimes dresses up as a man.

"Yes, it suits you."

A noisy, icy gust whooshes through the alley, lifting the bottom hem of my dress and dragging through my braided hair. I watch some flower petals fly out of my hair and glide with the cool wind. The flower petals scatter along the sandy ground of the alleyway, tumbling through the dirt.

"What a delightful ball!" A loud voice echoes through the alleyway, piercing through the wind and this moment between the dressmaker and me.

"Yes, a masquerade! How mysterious!" another voice exhumes.

I turn to look to where the voices are coming from, shrinking closer to the stone wall in hopes that I will not be seen. I wait, watching the pair pass the alleyway and disappear into the night before I turn back to Lady Pénquil beside me.

But she is gone.

Realisation hits: I am standing alone in an alleyway, in the dark – after having had a couple of drinks at the ball. If anyone saw me here, they would be very suspicious. Especially Prince Fraviné. Or my father. I need to get back to the ball. And I need to appear as if nothing of notice has occurred.

Feeling my hair, to ensure that I have not lost too many flowers, I am quick to straighten any fly-away hairs. I pat down the skirt of my dress, with the palms of my hands, flattening the fabric and tulle so that I do not appear fishy.

A few minutes go by, before I emerge from the alleyway. The street is quiet. The waves that crash on the rocky shore below the cliff-face to the west is the only sound, as I make my way through the town, towards the castle, where music can be heard resonating through the kingdom as I draw closer.

Chapter 13

The wind that washes over the sea is cool when I arrive at my chambers late that night. I let the door close behind me and lean my body against it. Something inside me feels warm and soft. My stomach and chest feel like they are made of pillows, my brain made of soup. Inebriation takes over my body and I lay on the floor, against the door, gazing up at the ceiling.

I remember Lady Pénquil's hands on my hips. The way she held me up when I was swaying from drinking too much champagne. I imagine her emerald eyes watching mine. I shiver at the memory of her shoulder against mine the dark, secluded alleyway.

Lady Pénquil is truly magic. No other woman has made me feel things like this. No one has ever made my stomach tingle with their touch, made my heart stagger with a single look, made my bones ache with an invigorating grin.

"Your Highness?" comes Hazel's voice from the other side of the door. "Do you need some assistance, getting ready to bed?"

I try to ignore Hazel's voice, remembering when Lady Pénquil disappeared from the alley and I had gone back to the ball. I joined a waltz, where I half-heartedly danced with many blond-haired men, who all smiled at me and made polite conversation. They called me beautiful, and I accepted their comments graciously, though, it was spiritless. Then I had danced with an impassive Prince Fravinè, who I knew had had too many drinks, because he stepped on my feet twice.

Towards the end, the queen, wearing an amethyst jewelled mask, had joined us on the dancefloor – which I assume is uncommon, because all guests stepped back to the outskirts of the ballroom to observe.

I watched as Queen Nyssra danced with her son. I watched him sweep her effortlessly, her black gown swishing violently over the floor. She twirled and turned in his arms, their eyes never leaving each other's.

Watching them dance together was captivating.

And when the song ended, all the guests clapped. The silver trays of food and champagne disappeared. The musicians began to pack up their instruments, and the queen thanked the guests for coming with a quick speech.

"We are grateful to have King Kelriaq and Princess Aruniar visiting our country. We are grateful to have abundant food and wine, to share with our visitors. And we are grateful to have allies, not only across the sea, but also right here in Whŷstelkiné. Thank you for attending our masquerade ball, and we look forward to hosting another very soon."

And with that, the queen disappeared from the ballroom. Her shiny shoes clicked noisily as she made her way to her chambers.

The guests were dismissed.

As the guests and musicians left the castle, Prince Fraviné started to wobble. He held a nearby stone pillar to prevent himself from landing face-first on the floor of the ballroom. The prince held a gasp on his mouth, and his shoulders quaked. He made rhythmic movements with his back, as he leaned on the pillar for support, a choking sound coming from him.

When I had asked him if he was all right, he waved me off, saying, "This happens often, my princess. Please let me be."

"I want to help," I argued.

"Please, Princess," he sighed. "This is humiliating enough."

With that, I sympathised. He was embarrassed by his drunkenness. He did not want to be sick in front of me, a lady. While I understood his intention, I did find it a little frustrating that he did not want my help. I would have been happy to comfort him – and I did not judge him for his intemperance; I would have been a hypocrite to judge, as I too was quite drunk.

So, I left him. I left the ballroom and began walking through the castle, stopping briefly on the stairs when I saw Justrikk, one of Prince Fraviné's lords-in-waiting, leaning against the outer wall of the balcony. He was holding a small roll of paper to his lips, and grey smoke twirled around his face, blowing in the breeze.

"Justrikk," I called to him through the window. "Justrikk!"

When he had heard me shouting, Justrikk nearly jumped out of his skin. He turned to look at me with a look of either shock or shame. I could not tell which.

"Forgive me, Your Highness! I was having a short break," he explained, his voice sounding guilty. He dropped the strange roll of paper on the stone floor of the balcony and stamped on it with his toes, hastily.

"The prince is inebriated," I told him, ignoring the fact that he was acting so suspicious. "He will need some assistance to get back to his chambers."

It took three lords-in-waiting to carry Prince Fraviné up the stairs. Although he had been joking and hollering happily at his servants, he was practically asleep by the time I heard the lords-in-waiting grow close to his quarters.

I had waited in the hallway outside of my chambers, listening for the lords-in-waiting to call out for help. They did not need assistance; however, I did hear much laughing and joking.

"He's drunk as a skunk!" Justrikk had told the others, chuckling.

"He's so heavy!" another complained.

"Oh, put your back into it, Hesbröwth," the third servant had commanded, though his voice was light-hearted.

"I'm trying!"

With a few more grunts, groans and hitches of hysterical laughter, eventually the servants got Prince Fraviné into his chambers, and the heavy wooden door snapped shut with a *click*.

"Princess Aruniar?" my lady-in-waiting calls through the closed door again, making me jump, bringing me back into the current moment, where I still lie on the bed in my chambers, my head swirling with inebriation.

"Yes?"

"Would you like some assistance getting changed, Your Highness?" she offers.

"No, thank you," I tell her. "Go and relax, Hazel."

I wonder if my drunkenness comes through in my voice, but I wouldn't dare ask. It might seem improper. But wouldn't unknowingly sounding drunk be more improper than inquiring about it?

"Are you sure, Your Highness?" she calls.

I strain noisily as I struggle to unfasten my corset. It ties at the back, and I can hardly reach. My shoulders ache as I try to pry the ribbons apart. My sputters and moans must carry through under the door because my lady-in-waiting appears and begins unpicking the bow as she stands behind me.

"Oh, Princess."

"Thank you," I sigh.

"How was your evening?"

"It was…"

My mind wanders to the dark alleyway. The memory of Lady Pénquil's arm touching mine makes my cheeks burn and I feel a strange tickle in my stomach. It's not unlike the pressure I felt earlier in the night, gathering in my organs, tearing at my lungs.

"It was wonderful," I tell her dreamily.

"See?" Hazel smiles as she begins loosening the laces on my corset. "I told you that the prince wouldn't be that bad! He was quite charming, wasn't he?"

"No!" I snort suddenly. "He was horrible! It was someone else I spent time with tonight."

"Who?"

"Lady Pénquil!" I whisper-shout, almost giddy.

The corset falls to the floor at my feet. My lady-in-waiting grabs my shoulder with her chubby hand and turns me around so that I'm facing her, wearing nothing but my undergarments and a sheer petticoat.

"A woman?" Hazel hisses at me. Her eyes are wide, and her face is so close to mine that I can smell alcohol on her breath.

"Yes," I reply simply.

"You spent the evening with a *woman*?" she repeats. Her eyes are wide, caramel irises are staring at me, shrining, narrowing, her gaze sweeping up and down my body. Something in the look that she gives me makes my heart quicken, my face warm.

The royalty in me wants to reprimand her for the tone she uses, but I cannot find the words. I simply stare at her, my hands balling into fists at my side.

Then she says, "What about the prince?"

"He's vile!"

"Irrelevant!" Hazel's tone is dismissive, not unlike my father. "That is not why we are here, Princess! We are here so that you may seduce Prince Frąviné! If you're not going to do that, this whole voyage was a waste of time!"

Suddenly, my inebriation disappears; I feel sobriety clear my head, and it is lit with outrage.

How does she have the nerve to speak to her princess that way? Perhaps, I have let her get away with too much. Perhaps, I have been too easy on her. What would my father say if he heard her speak to me this way? What would Prince Frąviné say?

"I do not care for that tone," I chastise firmly, brushing her hand off my shoulder.

Hazel freezes. Her gaze is steady on me as she takes a deep, cleansing breath. Returning to her task of undressing me, she is much calmer when she says, "I am just thinking perhaps you should spend a bit more time with the prince."

"Why? I already know that I despise him."

"You should not speak that way about your betrothed, Your Highness."

"He isn't my betrothed!"

"But he will be!"

"Why does he have to be?"

"Because!" She takes another deep breath, talking slowly as though she's thinking while she talks. "Maybe it would be in your best interest to marry the prince."

"I don't want to marry him!" I nearly shout. Then I catch myself and lower my tone. "I don't see why I must marry him, Hazel. He is awful."

Depleted and defeated, I slump down onto my bed. The springs bounce under my weight and my white, lacey petticoat puffs out around me with the speed of the motion. Sighing heavily, I bury my face in my hands, my fingertips cold on my cheeks.

Hazel sits beside me and pats my back. Her voice is gentle when she speaks again. "Your father has searched far and wide for a suitor your age. He has spent years looking for appropriate prospects."

"Years?"

"Years. Since you were a little girl."

Part of me feels a pang of guilt, but another part feels uneasy. It's a strange feeling to know that my father has been thinking about my marriage since I was a child. It feels unnatural. It feels creepy. There's something unpleasant about it. Something kind of vulgar.

"But... I was just a child," I protest, repulsed by the idea.

"This is about your future, Your Highness. The future of your country," she tells me, as though I've never heard this argument before. "Your father has always been thinking about your future."

"My future? You mean making alliances!"

"Alliances are very important," Hazel sighs exasperatedly. "You know this."

"To trade a daughter for alliance is sick!" I stand up from the bed so that I am standing in front of her. "What about my happiness? What about love?"

"*Love?*"

It's a single word, but there's so much raw shock and betrayal in Hazel's voice that it yanks at my chest and aches in my ribs. Our eyes meet and I feel my heart pounding hard in my chest. There's a hurt in Hazel's eyes that I can't really place.

"Is that all that you'll be needing tonight, Your Highness?" Her voice is cold, but I'm not sure why.

"Yes."

"Very well," Hazel says with a heavy exhale. "I shall be here early tomorrow morning to help you dress. The prince has a surprise planned for you."

When she's gone and the door is firmly closed behind her, I remove my petticoat and lie down the bed, wearing only my undergarments. The silk sheets are cool on my face, the air from the sea smells salty and I enter dreamland sooner than I planned.

***

When the sun streams in through the door to the balcony, it warms my face, turning my cheeks the slightest tinge of pink. Usually, it wouldn't bother me; I would turn over and go back to sleep for a couple of hours. But today, Hazel comes storming into my chambers. The heavy door closes loudly behind her as her shoes click on the stone floor.

"It's time to get up," she tells me firmly when I pretend to still be asleep. "The prince has a surprise for you."

It's when she begins talking that I feel a pounding in my head. It starts in the back of my brain and then moves to a more central part of my brain. At first, I wonder why I would be feeling so uncomfortable so early in the morning, but then my mind drifts back to last night, and I see flashes of the ballroom, several men chatting with me over champagne, a man in a black mask with a quirked smile and a dark alleyway. A man, who is a woman.

"Princess!"

I make a gruff groaning sound deep in my throat and shove my face further into the pillow. My breaths are heavy and nauseating as I respire into the stuffing of the silk cushion. I wonder if I will be sick.

"That is not the right attitude for such a romantic surprise, Your Highness," Hazel huffs. "Now, please get up."

She then pulls the silk covers off me, revealing my almost naked body underneath. The air is warm, compared to the cool sheets that enclosed me. As I roll over so that I am facing her, I see the angry line that creases her forehead between her eyebrows, and I feel the slightest touch of guilt fizzle in my chest. But then a wave of nausea washes over my body.

"Up!" Hazel orders. The urgency in her voice startles me and I jump. "We don't have long to get ready!"

"I don't even have a dress to wear!" I moan.

"The dressmaker brought some dresses to the castle while you were asleep." She gestures to a white box that I hadn't noticed her place on the bed when she first entered the chambers. "You have three choices."

Suddenly, I don't feel as sick. As I sit up and lean my back against the head of the bed, I catch a glimpse of myself in the full-length mirror that leans against the wall on the other side of the room, close to the bathtub. My hair is scruffy and frizzy, falling out of the loose braids that my lady-in-waiting had weaved the night before. My eyeshadow and liner are a black smear over my cheeks. What had once been neat red lipstick is now a single smudgy line that goes from the corner of my mouth to my chin. I'm a mess.

I wonder whether the prince would find me attractive if he saw me right now. A man has never seen me when I first wake in the morning. Would Prince Fra̧viné be repulsed by my disarray? Or would he still find me attractive? Would Lady Pénquil find me attractive?

That thought causes a warmth to grow in my stomach.

Hazel removes the three dresses from the box and lays them

neatly on the bed for me to observe. The first dress is a sky-blue maxi day-dress, with floral patterns and a thin white lace that trails along all the hems of the garment. The next is a knee-length velvet gown, a dark shade of orange, with a tulle pleated skirt and no sleeves.

In a much better mood now, I look over the options laid out on the bed as Hazel commences combing my hair. The comb tugs on my fizzy tangles.

Looking at myself in the mirror, only a few minutes later, I'm wearing the final dress that Hazel has removed from the white box. It's an earthy green coloured casual wrap-around dress that comes to my shins, made of a tablecloth-like material. It's nothing elaborate, but I do enjoy the fact that it is so unlike anything I would usually wear.

"All right, are you ready, Your Highness?" Hazel exhales as she opens the door to my chambers.

With one more spray of my signature vanilla and jasmine perfume, and one last look in the mirror, I am ready.

As we walk together through the stone corridor, there is not a sound but our footsteps that echo stridently through the quiet castle. Being early in the morning, I imagine that the rest of the residents of the castle as still asleep, curled up in their beds while I go to meet the prince for a secret surprise.

"Where are we meeting him?" I ask Hazel in a muted voice.

"The prince has asked me to bring you to the kitchens," my lady-in-waiting explains briefly as we start down the stone staircase. "He has said that he would like to share something with you."

Confusion clouds my thoughts as Hazel leads me through the ballroom and dining hall, our footsteps ringing throughout the castle, bouncing off the walls and high ceilings of this huge, empty palace. She knocks politely on the large wooden door to the kitchen.

When the door opens, Prince Fraviné is standing there wearing nothing but a pair of loose shorts. His golden curls are not combed, there's the slightest sward of light stubble around his mouth and chin, and his hairless chest and stomach are damp with beads of sweat.

"Good morning, my princess," Prince Fraviné grins broadly. His blue eyes look over me musingly, with a half-smile. "Please, come in."

When I follow the prince into the kitchen, Hazel is only a step behind me.

I've never been inside a kitchen before. There are benches on every wall, concrete beneath my sandalled feet, a silver sink on either side of the room and a few wooden stools around the island bench in the centre of the kitchen. Three blond-haired boys sit at the island bench, with a large silver mixing bowl between them.

"I invited my brothers," Prince Fraviné says with a chuckle. "We usually make breakfast together on Sundays."

"Really?"

I'm a little surprised by this news; I'd been under the impression that the prince didn't favour his brothers. His comment about there being "four left" was slightly concerning and although it hadn't been on my mind much, I am thinking about it now.

"We're making pancakes!" The little boy who says it can't be more than ten years old. He's holding a wooden spoon in one hand, and there's white flour on his nose.

The rest of the boys appear older; twelve, maybe fourteen years old. They don't seem nearly as excited about making pancakes as the youngest, which I find to be slightly humorous. Inside me, I feel something pull at my heart. A longing for a sibling.

"Do you like pancakes, Princess?" Prince Frąviné inquires.

"Yes," I answer.

"I like jam on mine," the youngest brother tells me happily, with glimmering blue eyes.

We spend the next forty-five minutes to an hour mixing the batter and making several batches of pancakes. There's a plate on the island bench between the brothers, where all the pancakes are placed when they are cooked. They don't stay on the plate long enough to be served; the children eat them faster than they can be cooked.

Prince Frąviné reprimands his brothers several times for eating the pancakes before they're served, but it doesn't stop them. Eventually, he gives up.

I feel a deep connection to the prince when he engages with his younger brothers. I wonder whether this affection is due to my envy for his closeness with his siblings, or if I am becoming more attracted to him.

When he and I are sitting at the table in the dining hall, a plate of pancakes between us, surrounded by whipped cream, fruits, a honey pot and a jar of unicorn apple jam, I feel weirdly fascinated by the prince. I watch him closely as he spreads jam onto a pancake in the palm of his hand.

"What?" He grins at me as he takes a bite, a little jam smearing on his top lip.

"Do you spend much time with your brothers?"

"Not really," he replies with a shrug. "They're kind of annoying, honestly. But they like being with me, and they're cute sometimes."

"They are cute."

"Do you have siblings?" He holds a pancake to my lips, and I take a bite of it.

"No," I say between chews.

"Why not?"

"My mother only wanted a single child, and my father was always away, travelling," I explain. "He wasn't home much when I was a young child."

"Are you close with your mother?"

I feel grief squeeze my chest. It singes the inside of my lungs and burns my throat when I breathe. My mother's face dances across my imagination, and I feel the nauseous feeling from earlier swirl in my stomach. Anguish swims in my heart and my mind and I wish, not for the first time, that my mother was here right now.

"She's dead."

"Oh, I'm sorry," he replies. "I didn't know."

"She died in childbirth when I was fifteen," I recall, sadness taking over my voice. "She didn't want another child, but she fell pregnant. The doctors said that it wouldn't be safe for her body, but she refused to give the baby up."

"And the baby?"

"Died."

"That must have been hard." The prince places his hand on mine, and as I look into his eyes, I feel the grief lift slightly.

"It still is, sometimes," I whisper. "My father was distraught. He was inconsolable for months."

"Are you and your father close?"

"Sort of. Not like I was with my mother. He was away a lot, and when my mother died, he spent most of his time alone." I look down at my lap and pick at my fingernails to distract myself. "My lady-in-waiting and I are close. She was my closest confidant for a very long time."

"Yeah, I understand that." The prince nods his head. "Our servants can feel like family sometimes."

"Hazel is more than a servant. She is my friend."

Prince Frąviné blinks at me. A smile tugs at his lip, and he waits for me to elaborate, as though he believes that I am joking. It's quiet for a second, before he pats my arm gently with the tips of his fingers.

"It might seem that way," he chortles. "But I doubt that she feels that way about you."

"Excuse me?"

"You are not her friend, Princess. You are her employer. If she wanted to, she could leave at any time."

"But she doesn't leave," I argue.

"Because you pay her."

"So?"

"So, she stays for the money, of course."

"So?"

"So, friends don't do that. Friends don't need to be paid to comfort and support you," the prince says slowly. "She isn't your friend."

I don't want to believe it. I want to tell him to shut up. I want to say that he is being ridiculous, and that my lady-in-waiting would never leave me. But suddenly, the uncertainty is overwhelming.

Is that why she didn't want to come to Whŷstelkiné? Was she going to disappear while I was gone?

Chapter 14

When the sun is setting that afternoon, I decide to go for a stroll by myself through the town square. Hazel offers to go with me, but I've been feeling insecure since my conversation with the prince this morning; it has my questioning things I had always known as fact before.

Is Hazel even my friend?

"Do you need some assistance, Your Highness?" Hazel asks me as I start to leave the castle. "I will accompany you, carry your bags for you."

"No, thank you," I decline.

"Are you sure? I don't have any chores right now," she argues, walking alongside me as I start down the castle steps.

"I'm fine."

"Your Highness, you really shouldn't be walking the streets at night by yourself," Hazel tries to stop me. "It's dangerous. What if something happens to you?"

"I'll be fine, Hazel." My voice is a bit harsh when I say it, but I am becoming frustrated, having to repeat myself. "Go back to the castle."

The streetlamps are glowing dimly in the square as I make my way down the dirt road, my shoes scuffing softly on the red sand beneath my feet. There's the smell of fresh bread in the streets. I can feel the gentle wind on my face, blowing my hair back and ruffling the skirt of my dress.

Several people are wandering around the street. Couples

walk together, holding hands and talking; a group of young women in casual dresses enter the tavern on my right; and several merchants are packing up their stores.

"Good evening, Your Highness," people greet in quiet tones as they pass me, keeping their heads down, not meeting my eye.

I'm reminded again of home. Back in Willcrest, people stop me in the street to talk. They often share stories with me, invite me to have dinner and offer me goods in the street. We share stories and food, as though we are one and the same, enjoying one another's company; not because I am the princess, but despite that. Things are so different here, where townspeople will not even look me in the eye when they speak to me, as though they are ashamed. Scared, even.

"Princess." It's a familiar voice that brings my eye from the ground at my feet to the green eyes that pour into me.

"Lady Pénquil," I greet happily.

She always makes eye-contact with me, like an equal. She never hides her face or stares at my feet when I speak to her; it makes me feel like she is genuinely happy to engage with me. And, at the moment, that is exactly what I need.

"Where are you headed at such a late hour?" she wants to know. There's a grin on her lips that makes my heart skip a beat.

How I admire her.

"I'm not sure," I reply honestly. "I was just going for a walk."

"I see."

"And where are you headed?"

"I've closed up my shop for the night, and I was going to the tavern for a drink," Lady Pénquil enlightens. "Would you like to join me?"

Do I want to join her? If these townspeople can't even meet

my eye in the street, how would they act when I have a drink in my hand? But then again... I would be with Lady Pénquil, and I quite like being with her.

"Yes, I think so," I decide.

Lady Pénquil looks delighted. A wide smile spreads across her face, causing little wrinkles in the outer corners of her eyes. She leads me across the street, to the windowed door of the tavern. The sign swings squeakily over the door, and the door jingles cheerily as we enter.

The inside of the tavern is lit dimly with iron chandeliers, and candles on small, round tables. There is hard-wood bar on the far side of the tavern, shiny under the hanging lights, with iron stools all the way along it.

I follow the dressmaker to the bar, where she jumps up onto a stool, her dress flowing out around her as she does. When I take a seat beside her, the man with a short beard behind the bar looks from Lady Pénquil to me briefly, before he asks us what we would like to drink.

"Oh, I don't know," I stutter nervously.

I've never been in a tavern before; back home, I would drink champagne and wine alone in my chambers. Sometimes I would sneak a sip of my father's beer, but I don't like it much; it's too bitter. What kind of drink could I order at a tavern?

"Two glasses of red wine," Lady Pénquil confidently tells the barkeep when I fail to answer. "Fill them all the way, please."

"All right," the bartender replies with a wink.

When he's off finding a bottle of wine, Lady Pénquil turns to me and leans her head on her hand on the bar. She's watching me closely as I look awkwardly around the tavern.

There are more people here than I imagined; it's not overly busy, but more than a few men and women are here, drinking liquor and eating meals at scattered tables. The hum of conversation is not overwhelming, but it's much less silent than outside in the street, where the only sound seemed to be the ocean waves.

"What do you think?"

"Of the tavern?" I clarify.

"I guess," she says with a shrug of her shoulders. "But also, Whŷstelkiné. Is it different from your home?"

"A bit." I nod.

The bartender places large glasses of red wine beside us. The mouth of the glass is larger than my fist. The shock must show on my face because Lady Pénquil starts laughing as she takes her first sip.

"What's wrong?" she wants to know.

"That's a lot of wine," I observe, keeping my voice low so that I don't offend the barkeep.

"It's not like the tiny champagne flutes at your balls, huh?" She's grinning widely at me, her green eyes on mine over the top of her glass.

"No," I agree.

"Taste it."

As I take the wineglass in my hand, I realise that I'm shaking a little. But it's not cold in here. Why would I be shaking? Does it have something to do with this prickly feeling that tremors my stomach and flitters inside my pelvis?

Bringing the glass to my lips, I take a sip of the red liquid.

"Do you like it?" Lady Pénquil asks me.

"It's different from the wine back home," I reply, placing the wineglass on the bar in front of me. "Sweeter. I think I like it better."

"What else is different about your home? You didn't finish

telling me."

"Well." I take a deep breath and look deeply into my glass of dark red wine. "It's… there's a lot more rainforest. No beaches in the kingdom, really."

"Really?"

"There's are ports for trade, but no beach. Our kingdom is much larger than this," I go on. "We have balls often. The most recent was one that I hosted for my birthday, and I love to invite everyone. Prince Frąviné said that that's something that doesn't really happen here."

"You're right," Lady Pénquil replies. "Most Whŷstelkinérs are not usually invited to balls or royal parties."

I don't know what else to say so, to avoid talking for a bit, I take another big gulp of my drink. It tastes like the pink tea that I've been drinking at the castle.

"Do you like it here?" she questions.

I swallow my mouthful. "I've been feeling a bit homesick."

"Oh, really? What's making you miss home?"

"I guess, everything is different here. I miss how things are back home."

"Yeah, I understand." Lady Pénquil nods, though, I don't know how she could understand, since this town is her home.

I change the subject: "Have you ever travelled?"

"No," she replies with a shake of her head. "I spend most of my time in my shop, which I love, don't get me wrong. But I do wish I could see more of the world. The furthest I've ever been is the mountains in the south-east."

I'm halfway done with my enormous glass of wine by now, but Lady Pénquil is drinking hers much faster – she's only got a couple of sips left.

"What's in the mountains?" I ask.

"Mostly forest."

"What do you do out there?

"Some go out there for spiritual alignment. There are gods out there, and some need to be in the forest to feel close to them."

"Is that why you went out there?"

Lady Pénquil considers me for a moment, her eyes fixed on mine. Her gaze is exact, complete, as though I'm a beguiling piece of parchment, and she's a scholar absorbed by the thrill of studying me. Then she softens, as though taking repossession of her composure. A smile tugs her thin, pink lip, and I feel an ache dull in my chest.

"You ask many questions, Your Highness," is all she offers.

She tips her glass up, polishing off her drink, before she gestures to the bartender to bring her another.

Seeing her finish off her beverage, I feel a little pressure to drink mine faster, but I do not let on. In fact, I try to keep the conversion – and my expression – as unruffled as normal. I would not want her to think that she has shocked me. A princess must keep her expression poised at all times.

"I'm simply curious," I say with a shrug, turning back to my own glass of wine. I take the tiniest sip, only to keep myself from saying any more; give her a chance to elaborate.

"I see."

There's a moment of silence. In this minute of stillness, I wonder whether Lady Pénquil will tell me anything at all. I wonder if I have overstepped. Perhaps this spiritual business is some sort of secret. Perhaps foreigners are not supposed to know about the mountains. That thought makes me more interested.

"What other secrets have you got to tell me?" I allow a little playfulness to slip through my flirtatious tone, though I am filled with genuine curiosity.

She regards me a moment, her gaze steady on mine, her lips

curled at the corners. Then, she says, "What would Her Highness like to know?"

I lean in close and whisper, "I'd like to know more about the prince."

Pénquil leans away from me wearily, her eyes narrowing. Perhaps she is afraid to discuss the royal family in such a public place.

"I've heard some untoward things about him," I add. "I hoped that you would provide some clarification."

For a second, Lady Pénquil just watches me. Her expression turns grave, her green eyes darkening. At first, I think she is not going to answer; that she will simply ignore my request.

"Well, I've told you before, Your Highness, that he is not kind," she says slowly and deliberately.

"I know," I nod. "I'd like to know more. Specifics."

"Have you noticed how he treats his staff?"

I think back to all the unnecessary requests he has demanded on Justrikk, his lord-in-waiting, the way he had laughed when his lord-in-waiting appeared afraid of him. A flicker of anger sparks in my stomach as I recall his dismissive tone towards Hazel, how he ordered her around as though she were his own servant.

"Yes."

"Well," she breathes. "I'm sure you have not seen the worst of it."

"What is the worst of it then?"

Lady Pénquil takes a breath, her chest and shoulders rising visibly as she does, as though she were almost scared. She reaches for her glass, now looking away from me. There is something in her eyes, something sombre and shaky, that makes me wonder whether the prince has been especially nefarious to her.

"Have you seen how he treats women?" she asks.

And I nod, because I have in fact seen the way he treats *me*, of all women.

"Prince Fr̦aviné is evil."

Well, that is no revelation.

"He is especially despicable towards women."

"He's sexist."

She shakes her head. "He is much more than that, Your Highness. He is cruel. He is… heartless."

"How so?"

"Let me ask you a question, Princess Aruniar," she says, now shifting in her seat. She is so close that I can smell the lavender scent of her shop on her clothing. "Are you always this curious?"

"Yes, but you are avoiding *my* question."

"Why do you think the prince is not married?"

"Pardon?"

"He is older than you, right? You're twenty-one, and he's what… twenty-five at least, I'm sure."

"So?"

"Don't you find that suspicious? A perfectly eligible bachelor, objectively, not unattractive, rich, a prince no less! And yet, he can't seem to find a wife. Why do you think that is?"

I do not answer.

"As the kingdom's most sought-after dressmaker, surely, I would hear every rumour in town! Don't you think I might have heard whispers about him, from duchesses and princesses alike?"

"What kind of rumours?"

"They say he is… indecent."

My stomach turns uncomfortably. "Indecent, how?"

"Have you seen any female staff at the castle?" She changes the subject so quickly that I pause to think.

I had not noticed, but she is right; all Whŷstelki̦nérs who work at the castle, except for Hazel, are men. In fact, I have not even seen the queen's lady-in-waiting. Does she even have one?

"Not apart from my own," I answer.

"And why do you think that is?"

"Perhaps because the prince was so horrible towards them?"

"Or, perhaps, because he cannot be trusted with them."

What does that mean?

But Lady Pénquil does not offer any clarification. She simply sips her second glass of wine. Her green eyes have shifted from mine, to look at something over my shoulder. There's a soft smile on her lips, a coy look in her eye.

When I turn to see what the seamstress could be looking at, my heart skips in my chest. My mouth goes dry. I feel a certain kind of discomfort bubble in my heart, and my cheeks warm with envy.

With that, I tip the last of my glass into my mouth and swallow it. I place the glass back on the table, Lady Pénquil's attention suddenly back on me. She watches me closely as I stand from the stool and smooth out my dress with my palms, making sure that it is not ruffled or looking as dishevelled as I feel.

"Where are you going?" Lady Pénquil asks me suddenly, as I start to leave.

"Thank you for the drink. I must head back to the castle now." I say this in the most pleasant and polite voice I can wrangle. "I shall be seeing you."

I even don't wait for her to reply before I leave the tavern, the bell on the door jingling, piercing my hearing as I go.

Outside, a light shower is drizzling in the street. The streetlamps are dim against the falling rain. The sky is black, from the night, but there are no stars, probably covered by dark storm clouds in the heavens.

As my shoes click loudly on the dirt road, I wrap my arms around myself, shielding as much of my body from the downpour as possible.

There are several servants locking the front doors of the castle when I get there. Each of them looked as shocked as each other, as I approach them. Their stunned faces make me question what I must look like; my braided black hair, probably frizzing from the rain, my dark skin gleaming wet, don't even get me started on my dress – it's probably ruined!

The sound echoes through the castle halls, as I slam the door to my chambers, the iron latch on the door rattling loudly as it settles in place.

As I lie in bed, I think of Lady Pénquil, the look on her face as she peered over my shoulder. That flirty expression, not aimed at me, but a Whŷstelkinér. With long, blonde hair and captivating grey eyes, mild features, a round and delicate face the colour of parchment, her thin lips stained with red from her wine.

I had been so sure that Lady Pénquil and I had had a connection. In that alleyway, it had felt like we were the only two people in the world. Did she not feel that way?

Chapter 15

For two days, the rain doesn't stop. It drizzles miserably outside the castle. This downpour seems never-ending. The sky is a dark shade of grey, the clouds a swirling black, churning over the kingdom, bringing cold, howling winds from over the sea. The gale gusts through the castle, yowling like a wrathful phantom.

Although many Whŷstelkinérs are game enough to walk the streets, carrying on their business as usual, my father and I spend the two days locked away in the castle. My father sits to the right of Queen Nyssra, who often has a fragile teacup in her hand, filled to the brim with pink tea. The queen patiently listens to my father, who shares many stories of when he was a voyager. She never seems to tire of his tales, always watching him carefully with deep green eyes, focused, as though he were the most stimulating creature in the world.

I don't feel that way; my father's stories are tiresome, and my father even more so. After an hour of listening to his tedious tales on the first day of the storm, I stomp out of the room, heading back to my chambers, to be alone. A prince stops me on the way, asking where I am headed, as though it is not so obvious. His features are so similar to Fravine's, that if I did not know for a fact that my betrothed is much taller, I might have gotten them confused.

"Back to my chambers," I reply slowly.

"Would you like to go for a walk?" the teenage prince asks me.

"Sure."

As we walk through the castle, the rain a hushed spatter on the roof, high above us, I start to wonder if I even know which brother I am walking alongside. Looking at his face is no help; all these Whŷstelkiné princes look the same, with their blue eyes and sandy hair. In fact, perhaps the only thing that separates them is their age.

"I'm sorry," I tell him gently as we take a seat on a balcony that overlooks the rose garden. "Not to sound rude, Your Highness, but I'm not sure which prince you are."

Where I had expected the young prince to be offended, he shocks me with a snort of amusement. I could say that I am relived, but I am also very wary.

"I get that a lot. My brother loves to be the centre of attention. We rarely get a look in. I'm Prince Novaāke."

"Lovely to officially meet you," I say with a charming smile.

"I understand that you are here to capture my brother's heart," Prince Novaāke tells me simply. Whatever he wants to talk about, it is clear to me that he is cutting right to the chase.

"I suppose so."

"Why?"

"Well, my father believes that Prince Fraviné and I are a good match," I try to explain.

"King Kelriaq had never met my brother until you arrived on our shores," the young prince argues. "How could he have known that you were a good match for my brother?"

There is a sort of protectiveness in his voice that makes me thoughtful. Why would a younger brother feel so protective over an older brother? Why might Prince Novaāke believe it his job to be cautious on his older brother's behalf?

"I'm not sure." I speak slowly and carefully. "Perhaps my

father knew your parents, back when he was a voyager."

"Perhaps. But why would that make you a decent match?"

"Maybe my father knew what kind of boy Queen Nyssra would raise," I offer.

"Perhaps."

There is silence between us for a few moments. Although we don't speak, it is not silent. The waves crash to our east, the wind bellows all around, the rain continues to fall from above, just as heavy as it had for the entire day.

"Why are you so curious, anyway?" I challenge.

"My brother is... well, he's a romantic, at heart," Prince Novaãke explains to me. "Given the chance, Frąviné would marry for love – rather than politics."

Now I understand. Prince Novaãke does not want his brother marrying for political gain, but for love. It is not a political match that Prince Novaãke was inquiring about, but a love match. All these questions are to suss out whether I was in love with the Prince of Whŷstelkiné, and why I intend to marry him.

But what would Prince Novaãke do with this information? If he knew that I did not love the prince, that I was not even remotely attracted to Prince Frąviné, what might he say? What might he do? Would he tell the queen? Would he tell my father?

Then Prince Novaãke asks a more specific question: "After only having been here a week, you couldn't know that you love him, could you?"

I choose my words carefully when I tell him, "It doesn't seem long enough."

"I agree."

"Perhaps, I could extend my stay," I offer as a solution. "Then I could know for sure what my feelings are for Prince Frąviné, and whether we would be a good match."

He nods his head slowly, as though he were a medium, reading a prophecy. "Perhaps. Or, perhaps, we know the answer already."

"Do we?"

"I think we do."

At first, I wonder what he could mean. At first, I think that perhaps he is tricking me. Perhaps he is using some sort of reverse psychology to get me to disclose that I, in fact, do not like the prince in any sense.

Then, he says, "Do you lay with women?"

And my heart stops.

Prince Novaãke and I hold eye-contact for the longest time. His ocean-blue eyes drill into me, daring me, challenging me. His lips are a firm line, unmoving, unsmiling. The look on his face is so solemn that it makes me uneasy. My stomach coils and my chest pinches. The look on his face causes an anxious and fearful sensation inside me, as though I have been caught stealing gold coins from a maiden's purse. What would he do if I told him the truth?

"I have never laid with a woman," I tell him truthfully.

Now the straight line of his thin lips becomes a tickled smile. He lets out a soft breath of amusement, one of his gold eyebrows raised in a quizzical sort of way, and he shakes his head, as though he doesn't believe me. Then he looks at my eyes again.

"You know I can see it in you, right?" he muses.

"Pardon?"

See it? How could he see it? This is not a thing you could physically see; it is invisible, a feeling deep inside. A tickling sort of sensation that lives far beneath my skin, and only arises when Lady Pénquil, the magic woman, touches me.

"I can see it. I recognise it."

Recognise it? How? What could this feeling possibly look like? How could he possibly know my own private thoughts? Does anyone else see these thoughts?

"All right," he sighs when I don't say anything. "I'll make you a deal."

"What kind of deal?"

"You don't want to marry my brother," he begins, and when I start to protest, he holds up a ceasing hand. "And I don't want you to marry my brother. My brother deserves to marry for love, and frankly, so do you."

It is strange to hear someone say that. Both Hazel and my father have been so set on me marrying the prince, so against my thoughts of marrying for love, that I never truly believed that it would happen. But right now, hearing Prince Novaãke speak about my *deserving* love, I can't help hoping.

"So, it seems that we have the same goal, correct?"

I could say: No, I want to marry Prince Fraviné. I could say: You have me all wrong, I like men. I could say: How do you know that I like women?

But I don't say any of those things. Instead, I say, "Correct."

The next day is Sunday, and the rain has stopped for now. It's dinnertime, and there is a large fish upon a silver platter in the centre of the enormous dining table. The meat smells of gravy and rosemary. Several side dishes, including potatoes, squash, green vegetables and what can only be described as mushed-up red fruits, are spread over the table.

The soft rumble of conversation fills the air, with eight people at the dining table. With Queen Nyssra at the head of the table, my father sits in his usual place, a pile of seafood on his plate, to the right of the queen. To her left are three of her children, their plates being made by a skinny-looking servant. Then there is Prince Frąviné, who sits directly across from me, piling potatoes onto his plate and drowning them in sauce. Between us, on my right side, is Prince Novaãke, who stabs aggressively at his green vegetables with a silver fork.

This is, perhaps, the noisiest table I have ever had the pleasure of sitting at. It's loud, but also welcoming. It's warm and familiar. Although the kingdom of Nashwalte is very far away, for a moment, this table feels like home. Children gathered around a table, sharing stories of their day, eating a meal that was prepared by several servants, a dining room warmed by the cracking fireplace, the prince looking at me from across the table – this could be my home. This could be my kingdom.

Then, as Prince Novaãke and I make brief eye-contact, I am reminded of the deal he and I had made the previous day. I am to repel the prince. I am to appear unattractive, repulsive, so that Prince Frąviné will choose another – then I will be free to marry whomever I choose.

With the plan in mind, I use my hands to pick up shredded slithers of meat from my plate. Vaguely, I hear the table chatter soften – but perhaps I am imagining it – and I look around the table.

All eyes, apart from the two youngest princes', are on me.

With the meat in my hands, I hesitate. The meat is soft. It is slightly greasy. I have never touched meat with my bare hands, especially not fish. It is unbecoming. My mother would swoon if she were at the table with us now.

When I was a child, my mother would tell me, "Aruniar, it is important that a princess is charming. That she is polite. Are you being polite, Aruniar, Princess of Nashwalte?"

She usually said this to me when I was doing something

distasteful or unladylike – like what I'm doing right now, with oil and fish juices dripping down my hands and wrists, the soft meat squishing noisily between my fingers.

Do it, I tell myself. *Or you'll have to marry Prince Frąviné.*

Desperate to appear unattractive to the prince, I put the whole fistful of meat into my mouth. It's a bit too much to fit, and for a moment, I panic. But then I force it, smearing oil around my lips and on my chin.

Five pairs of eyes watch as I chew my mouthful. I make eye-contact with each staring person at the table: my father, who looks as though I have slapped him; Queen Nyssra, clutching her chest with a face frozen in shock; the prince's second-youngest brother has a look of horror plastered across his narrow features, as though he has seen a ghost; Prince Novaăke, who is holding back a burst of laughter with a hand over his mouth and jaw.

And Prince Frąviné. His expression, though obviously dissatisfied, is unreadable. His sapphire eyes glare into mine. His mouth unmoving. His jaw is firm and set. His gold eyebrows slightly angled, but not furrowing like my father's.

No one speaks. No one breathes. It is pure silence as I chew my mouthful of meat, now staring directly into Prince Frąviné's eyes, waiting for him to talk. Oil seeps around my lips, and drips down my chin. In a frantic effort to appear undesirable to the prince, against all instinct, I allow the small drops of oil to trickle down my chin and drop into my lap.

After a moment, Prince Frąviné clears his throat. He turns his attention back to his sauce-soaked potatoes and commences eating his meal, perhaps with even more civility and grace than before. For a few seconds, his utensils are the only ones to scrape the porcelain plates.

As I look at him now, across the dining table, that inscrutable expression still evident on his features, I'm reminded of that offhanded comment Prince Frąviné had made on the first night in Whŷstelkįné.

Four brothers left.
Still, I wonder what that could have meant.

Later that night, I am sitting by a large window in the library, reading an enchanting book about a romance between two unlikely lovers, when none other than Prince Frąviné enters, wearing only a loose-fitting pair of slacks that sit lazily on his hips. The rain still pours, spattering on the glass of the window as I continue reading, pretending not have noticed his presence.

After a moment, the prince takes a seat on the velvet couch, perching himself right at the corner, as though he were afraid to sit on the chair.

"I cannot sleep," he informs me.

"Is that so?" I do not look up from the book I am reading, not giving him the satisfaction of interrupting me.

"We've angered him," Prince Frąviné tells me in a hushed tone.

"Who?"

"Eéijrwărpmąs, the Sea Beast."

"Oh, right." I laugh as I put my book down, entertained at his senseless superstitions. "And what exactly did we do to upset him?"

"I think he is frustrated with the foreigners on our land."

It occurs to me that perhaps Prince Frąviné uses this tale of the sea beast to make his own beliefs and desires known. It makes me even more curious.

Do other Whŷstelkįnérs believe this nonsense? Or has Prince Frąviné made it up purely for my benefit?

Either way, I must say, it has me rather intrigued.

"What can we do?"

"I think Eéijrwărpmạs wants me to decide fairly swiftly whether I shall marry you," the prince explains. There's an urgency to his voice, and I wonder if he believes his own lies.

"Well, have you decided?" I inquire.

"You shall be notified when that information becomes relevant to you."

And just like that, I am dismissed.

That is when a fire really burns in the pit of my belly: there are too many secrets in this kingdom, too many whispers, too many rumours. I intend to uncover them.

Chapter 16

I wait there, completely silent, until the prince is out of sight. When his footsteps are no longer audible in the echoing hallway, and all the lights in the castle are out, leaving the first floor of the castle a dark fortress of silence, I know that it is safe to leave my book while I sneak around to get some answers.

I walk slowly and carefully, tip-toing as quietly as I can manage. With just the candle I was using to read my book in the library, it's difficult to see my way, so I touch my hand to the wall to steady myself.

Aside from the waves that crash against the cliffs on the west side of the castle, not a sound can be heard. It's almost a little eerie, walking through a silent castle in pure darkness. I strain my ears to listen, but I am met with silence, so I assume that everyone is in bed.

I try the first door. The handle is cold, made of iron, and stiff in my hand. It rattles very slightly when I try to open it, but the door does not budge. It's locked.

My cheeks warm, but I move on, my mind set on finding out the answers to my questions.

I try the next door. I expect it to be locked as well, but it isn't. It swings open, the hinges whining softly.

As I step inside, my arms prickle with goosebumps, the hairs on my arms standing up as the cold wind from the sea whooshes in through the open window. The candle flickers slightly in the wind, and I raise my hand to protect the flame.

Inside the room, it smells of salt and candle wax. There is a large oak desk in the centre of the room, accompanied by a cushioned chair and matching footstool. The desk is littered with papers, candles, quills, ink pots, wax seals and leather-bound books. There is so much to take in that I don't know where to start.

Placing the candle on the flat surface of the desk, I begin looking over the pile of papers left on the desk. My eyes dart over the scrawled letters. Between ink blots and dirty fingerprints, I must squint to make out some of them.

The first is correspondence between Queen Nyssra and someone from Hupplerook, a continent to the north of this tiny island. Something about trade. Something about land. The proposal of allyship. Nothing useful. Nothing about Prince Fraviné.

The next paper I find is a hand-drawn map of the island. Someone has drawn thick crosses over certain places in the forest to the south-east of the kingdom. There are no labels. Just crosses, with no explanation of their meaning. Probably nothing.

Having no luck so far, I decide to search the drawers of the desk. The first drawer is stuck, firmly closed, barely moving when I tug at it. Both hands around the small, wooden knobs, I wrench the drawer open with a *crack*.

It's filled with letters. Hundreds of them. Some are addressed to the queen, while others are addressed to Prince Fraviné. I skim as many as I can, not bothering to read them fully, but when I discover that they are useless, I toss them aside.

Then, at the bottom of the drawer, hidden beneath all the other letters, I find a letter addressed to the King of Whŷstelkiné.

My heart stops in my chest as I look at the letter, the parchment thin in my hands, yellow with age. The lettering is thin and loopy. It looks like someone was in a rush to write it.

I sit in the chair as I read.

It's a letter written over twenty years ago.

Whoever wrote it confesses to stealing a child, but with no remorse. They claim that it was in the child's best interest, that the queen would make an appalling mother, how she is the most dangerous creature to plague the earth. They make several threats to the royal family, including death, if they try to find the missing child.

The letter is very clear, the meaning evident.

Whoever wrote this letter is very angry.

As I continue searching through the desk, I find another letter addressed to the prince. I toss the first one aside. Then I find another. And another. Another and another. A dozen, at least.

Unopened, still sealed.

I pause, looking to where I have cast them aside, thinking. In the pile on the desk, now over a hundred gathered there, a thought occurs to me.

Why wouldn't the prince open these?

Slowly, I pick the letters up, looking at them more closely. I turn them over in my hands, inspecting them. I compare the letters. They are all written in different handwriting, return addresses from all over the world. Some are even sealed with house seals from royal families.

When I open the first letter, I see that it is written by a young duchess from Losummit, one of Nashwalte's closest island neighbours. The letter starts off polite, asking how the prince is, how his kingdom is faring. But, as I read on, my eyes widen in shock.

I suddenly feel sick to my stomach.

My fingers tremble as I unseal the next letter. It is from another noble woman, this time a princess from Rosestone, a kingdom in the far east. Princess Chariyka. She writes with urgency. Her letter is pleading, begging the prince to admit to what he has done.

I hear my heart pounding in my ears as I scramble to grab yet another letter, this one from another princess from another continent. Then another, and another.

Each letter is written by a woman taken advantage of by the prince himself. Each woman turned down Prince Fraviné's hand when he proposed to them. Each woman is pregnant with his child. A child that he will never admit to fathering.

If I value my life as it is, I know that I must flee Whŷstelkiné.

***

In the morning, Hazel combs my hair and asks me why I haven't spoken to the prince today, but I just shrug. I haven't told her about the hundreds of letters I have hidden in the top draw of my wardrobe, and I don't plan to. I know what she would say. She would tell me that I am being ridiculous, that engaging in gossip about my future husband is dishonourable.

But she didn't see the letters!

"Are you okay, Your Highness?" she asks me. "You look tense."

I blink suddenly, coming back to reality, and realise that my hands are hard fists in my lap, my muscles tight on my arms and legs. My nails have left throbbing impressions on the palms of my hands.

"I'm fine." I take a deep breath, telling myself to relax.

"All right," she sighs, clearly not believing my lies. "Do you have plans for today? The sun is out. We could go to the market?"

"No," I say a little too quickly.

Hazel squints at me.

"I'll just stay in and read today," I tell her. "I didn't finish the book I was reading last night, and I simply must know how it ends."

"Of course." She nods.

Hazel re-braids my hair into neat and tight rows, weaving several gold and silver beads into my plaits, which perfectly match my silver bangles and earrings. This is something that Nashwaltians have done for generations; women braid flowers and beads into their hair, purely for beauty – not as sign of status or wealth. It's traditional for Nashwaltian women to wear their hair in braids. Not only does it tame our unruly curls, but it also helps to protect them.

In the hours that follow, I try to put as much distance between me and the prince as possible. When he approaches, I duck into the hallway, or turn around and walk the other way; I avoid him like the plague. Whether he notices or not, I do not know, but I cannot risk being caught – and I do not trust myself not to say anything about what I know, and I trust the prince even less.

I try to read in the Castle Library, like I told Hazel I would, but after several close calls with the prince, I know that I cannot keep my rage contained, so I head into town alone.

I notice again how nervous the Whŷstelkịnérs are in my presence; how shy they are. They bow their heads when I pass, they skirt around me as though I were an untamed horse, unpredictable and dangerous. They don't dare to meet my eye.

Their uneasiness makes me question their leadership. It makes me wonder what the monarchy has been like on this island, for its people to respond this way to royalty. It makes me curious – and it makes me angry.

One little girl with yellow pig tails stops at her mother's side as I pass. She drops a ball she has been carrying, which rolls across the dusty road and bounces into my heeled shoe. I stoop to pick up the ball for the little girl, but she has run to hide behind her mother before I can give it back to her.

"I apologise, Your Highness," the mother begins saying, her blue eyes wide and worried, her voice frightened. "Please forgive her. She is a child. I shall reprimand her when I get home."

"No," I try to say. "It is not—"

"Come on," the mother is saying, now dragging her daughter by the hand as they continue down the dirt road.

It is heartbreaking, and I find myself wishing for home.

Now standing alone in the street, several Whŷstelkĭnérs pass me, each of them eying me wearily as they walk by. I feel watched. I feel self-conscious. I wonder why the mother had a reaction like that to a simple mistake.

"Princess Aruniar."

It's a voice I know. One I am grateful to hear. When I turn, I see Lady Pénquil, who is holding an armful of fabrics and a wide smile on her face. Her green eyes peer into mine and I feel a warmth surge through my chest and heart.

"Lady Pénquil. How nice to see you."

"And you," she replies politely, though her eyes drill into me, something like interest plastered on her expression. "What might you be doing in town, without your servants?"

"Hazel is quite busy, and I wanted to explore alone."

"I see."

"What are you doing in town?" I eye her fabrics. "Are these for other clients?"

"Well, you've been to see me quite a few times," Lady Pénquil says with a dull laugh. "I needed to replenish my stock; you see. I was running out of my favourite fabrics."

"I understand."

"What are you planning on exploring in town?"

"I don't have a plan."

"Would you like a guide?"

"Aren't you busy?"

"I've had a foreign princess buy many of my garments over the last week or so, so I can afford to close my shop for a day." There's a smile on her lips and a knowing look in her eye and the memory of her pressed up against me in the alleyway replays in my mind. It makes my stomach twist.

"A guide would be lovely."

Lady Pénquil shows me the best place in town to find perfumes and scented oils. We eat fresh bread from the bakery. She takes me to a garden, where many children are climbing the trees and running around a green meadow, playing some version of tag I have never seen.

We sit on a bench at the edge of the garden, watching the children play. While we sit, Pénquil talks about Whŷstelkiné traditions, and the many kinds of things they do to keep busy during the day. At one point, she picks a pink flower from a nearby flowerbed and places it in my hand.

"It's a peony," she tells me with a smile. "Do you have these flowers back home?"

"Not this colour," I answer. "Most of our flowers are blue or purple."

Before I know it, we are walking again. Eéijrwãrpmas, it seems, is not some figment of Prince Fraviné's imagination, but a belief of the entire kingdom. She is telling me about a festival the town must celebrate the grace of Eéijrwărpmąs and his promise to never flood Whŷstelkįné again.

"Has it been flooded before?" I ask.

"Eéijrwărpmąs flooded Whŷstelkįné during a revolution," Lady Pénquil explains evenly, as she looks over the ocean. "He didn't approve of citizens rising up against the monarchy."

Lady Pénquil walks beside me. Her shoulder occasionally brushes mine, sending electric waves of excitement down my arm. She stops at the edge of a cliff that overlooks the ocean, on the west side of the island. This cliff, I will later learn, is called Eéijr Point. It wasn't always the edge of the city; apparently the kingdom used to be much larger, but with the storm that caused the flood, much of the island eroded away.

"There was a revolution?" I question.

"Nearly," Lady Pénquil shrugs. "The flood caused a lot of death in our city, and I guess with their grief, our people were too tired to fight. And the revolution ended. Now the monarchy reigns with no question of our loyalty."

I learn that Eéijr is the Whŷstelkįnér word for storm; Wărpmąs means monster. I learn that the sea monster is basically a god, in the eyes of a Whŷstelkįnér. Like the Gods of Life and Death, Whŷstelkįnérs believe that Eéijrwărpmąs holds their fate in his hands.

I understand now that the people are afraid. Their faith leads them to believe that Eéijrwărpmąs, the sea monster, will kill their families in a horrific storm, if they rise against the monarchy.

Perhaps that it why they are so afraid of me. Perhaps I remind them of their fragility against the monarchy. The monarchy that I now know is even more corrupt than it seems.

Chapter 17

In the following days, I feel my anger growing, cutting through my lungs with every breath. I try to control it. I try to tell myself that I have to bide my time. I just have to make sure that he is repulsed by me, so that he will not try anything. With any luck, in a few days, I will be on my way home.

But each time I look at him, I feel an uncomfortable knot in my stomach, knowing what he's been accused of, knowing what I know about him now. When he comes close to me, I back away, leaving a step or two between us. He doesn't seem to notice.

The next ball is going to be a black and white themed one. Prince Fraviné is sure that all his guests must come dressed in black or white, or both. He seems thrilled when he meets me in my quarters the very next day.

"You shall wear blue," he tells me decidedly.

"But it's a black and white ball," I argue plainly. "Won't I look out of place?"

"Precisely."

"I don't have a blue dress, Your Highness," I tell him.

"Well, then you have a day to prepare."

Oh, he is loathsome. How I would enjoy tossing a glass of red wine on a white shirt of his. How I would love smashing his face into a cake. How I would...

My thoughts are interrupted by the slamming of the door of my chambers, as Prince Fraviné leaves. The loud echoes of his quick footsteps can be heard stamping for ages down the dark stone hallway, and my mind swims with hatred for him.

"I need a black dress!" I announce as I enter the Modiste, the door closing firmly behind me.

Something makes me stop. An odour. A scent. A perfume, perhaps? It smells floral. It seems strange... And then there's smoke. Not a lot. Just one thin, grey cloud, twisting and gyrating in the air as it wafts through the dress shop.

Is something on fire?

"Lady Pénquil?" I call.

As I walk slowly and carefully through the Modiste, weaving between mannequins and dresses, I see that the smoke seems to come from the dressing room. It's a single cloud of smoke, fluttering over the door.

"Lady Pénquil, is that you?" I try again, now using two fingers to knock gently on the door to the dressing room.

The smell is much stronger here. It's a flowery scent, as though I were standing in the middle of the royal rose garden.

Then the door opens, and there is Lady Pénquil, sitting on the floor, dressed in a white blouse and brown skirt that reaches her knees. Her eyes are glassy, slightly pink in the corners, and she offers a half-smile. The thin trail of smoke rises from behind her head, but she appears not to notice it.

"Princess Aruniar," the dressmaker says flatly. "What can I do for you?"

"I need a dress," I explain.

"I see," Lady Pénquil says with a sigh. "Well, I'm having a short break. You'll have to come back later."

"I don't have time," I argue. "The ball is tonight."

"And?"

"Well, I don't have an appropriate dress," I tell her hastily.

"I'll pay you double. I just really need a dress for the ball, and I need it for tonight."

"I am on a break."

"Yeah, I understand that. But this is time sensitive. I only have until tonight to have something," I tell her stubbornly. "Please help me."

"Fine," she sighs.

Lady Pénquil holds out her hand to me, and instinctively, I take it. Her hand on mine makes my fingers tingle with electricity. I look in her eyes, and she offers me a smile. With trembling limbs, I pull her to her feet. Only when she is standing beside me do I consider whether that was an appropriate thing for a princess to do.

"I don't have time to make something from scratch," she explains, walking away from me, towards the racks of dresses. "What colour are you wanting?"

"The prince wants me to wear blue, but I want to wear black."

"You'll wear black, then."

The dressmaker sorts through the dresses on the racks, peering at each one closely, although, many of them are not black in colour. I notice now that there's something different about the way she walks; it's not like walking at all, in fact, more like floating. Poorly. She stumbles often, clutching the racks and dresses, wobbling on her feet.

Is she drunk? It's early in the day for alcohol.

"Are you all right?" I ask her.

"Quite."

"Is something wrong?"

"Why would something be wrong?" she questions.

"You seem… different."

Exasperatedly, she waves me off, as though my concerns are moderately bothersome to her. The action seems to knock her off-balance. With a shriek, Lady Pénquil claws at the air, her legs unsteady beneath her as she tumbles backwards. Before I can stop myself, I step forward, grabbing her shoulders as she staggers, catching her before she falls to the floor.

"Your Highness, I am sorry!" she exclaims, starting to push me off her.

"It's all right." Keeping my voice steady, despite the butterflies swarming inside my stomach, is extremely difficult. It's almost as difficult as not staring at Lady Pénquil's lips when she speaks. "Are you okay?"

"I'm fine," she assures me.

Within a couple of minutes, we have found a black, floor-length gown made of linen. Although it is not the most elegant of fabrics, Lady Pénquil guarantees that when she is done adding black lace, it will look exquisite.

After trying on the dress, Lady Pénquil makes the necessary adjustments, so that it will fit snuggly, and then she helps me back into my day dress. For the first time, I am embarrassed to have another woman see me in my undergarments.

"How about a cup of tea?" she offers.

"What about the dress?"

"I'll have it finished in time," she promises.

"I'm sorry you have to see me like this," Lady Pénquil sighs as she takes a seat at the table across from me a little white later. She rests her head on her hand as she leans on the table, rubbing one eye with the palm of her hand. "I wasn't expecting any customers today."

"What were you doing?" I ask.

She sips her tea from a teacup, eyeing me closely. "Who wants to know?"

"Me, obviously."

"What do you think I was doing?" she questions.

This conversation has already become infuriating.

What is she hiding? What was that strange-smelling smoke in the Modiste? Why does she reek of it?

"You must not tell Prince Fraviné," she whispers to me.

"Trust me," I snort. "I will not be telling that man anything. He is repugnant."

"On that, we agree."

Our eyes meet and we watch each other for a long moment. She starts off with a cunning expression, which quickly turns secretive. I feel my heart race in my chest when her pink tongue touches her bottom lip – perhaps licking at a drop of tea, or perhaps...

"Do you remember when we spoke about the mountains?" She places her teacup down on the table between us, the flirtatious moment apparently having passed. "Do you remember how I said that we go there for spiritual alignment?"

"I remember."

"The smoke... can... assist." It's as though she is choosing her words carefully, thinking while she speaks.

"The smoke?"

"Yes," Lady Pénquil whispers firmly. "The smoke opens the mind. It helps to heighten the senses. It... is a spiritual experience."

"How so?"

"Many believe that it helps to interact with the gods," she shrugs. "I don't, but many do."

"So, why are you so secretive about it?"

"Well, it's very valuable."

"So?"

"As far as I know, the royal family doesn't know anything about it," Lady Pénquil explains. "If they did, do you think they would be sharing it with us?"

I stare at her blankly. Perhaps she is right; before I suggested it, Prince Fraviné was not interested in having townspeople invited to balls. In a classist society, it's understandable that perhaps citizens would be opposed to having their rulers know of treasured objects. If they are indeed valuable.

"How is it valuable?" I ask.

"Let's just say… Whŷstelkiné is a much more… pleasant place, with this particular smoke," she says in a hushed tone. She speaks slowly, carefully, her eyes intense as they look in mine.

Is this a riddle of some sort? Why do I not understand what the dressmaker is trying to say? Why doesn't she just come out and say it? And why must she whisper? If Lady Pénquil knows about it, surely the other townspeople do as well.

"How so?"

"This smoke changes your perception. It can make you feel calm and happy. It can make you less stressed or worried. It can have stronger effects on you."

Now it makes sense.

"Like alcohol," I observe.

"Exactly."

"And why wouldn't you want the queen to know about it?" I ask her. "If it's so valuable, wouldn't you be able to sell it? Wouldn't the royal family pay a lot of gold for something like that?"

Lady Pénquil shakes her head. "The queen is not the problem. Don't get me wrong, she is horrible. But not like the prince."

"Prince Fra̧viné?"

"Yes."

"Well, what would he do?" I question. "There's a tavern. There's alcohol. Why not a little smoke?"

"The wine in the tavern is not alcoholic, Your Highness," Lady Pénquil explains. "Townspeople do not have access to alcohol in Whŷstelkiné – except for at their balls of recent."

I squint at her, thinking. "Why wouldn't the royals want the people to have alcohol?"

"Perhaps they are afraid of their people."

I think back to my time in the market in the previous days. I remember how Whŷstelkinérs don't look me in the eye; how they shrink away when I approach; how a mother promises to reprimand her child for dropping a toy at my feet. Royals that inspire that much fear would not be afraid of their own people, would they?

"That doesn't make any sense."

I take my first sip of the tea Lady Pénquil has made for me. My nose wrinkles at the taste. Its flavour is bitter, kind of sour even. Nothing like the sweet tea made from rose petals in the castle.

"What is the tea made from?" I ask, trying to sound curious rather than repulsed.

She grins, watching me over her own cup of tea. "It is not as good as the tea you've had in the castle, is it?"

"No."

"Perhaps that is because the royal family keeps everything of value to themselves."

And that, I think, is an interesting point.

Chapter 18

That evening, as I stand at the centre of the staircase leading to the ballroom, my back dress cascading down three stairs, many Whŷstelkinérs enter the castle, all dressed in black or white. There is a cool wind gusting in from over the sea. Salty and familiar, it fills the castle, lays a layer of glistening, warm salt upon my skin.

At the top of my head, I wear my mother's pearl tiara, the one that Prince Frąviné had told me not to wear in his kingdom. It gives me great satisfaction to feel the way the band sits firmly around my scalp, to see it twinkling in the reflection of my champagne glass.

My cup of champagne bubbles and fizzes against the glass. My lipstick has left a red smudge on the side of flute. In the reflection of the glass, I can see Prince Frąviné over my shoulder, coming down the stairs to the left. My breath shudders, but I keep my expression steady.

"Princess Aruniar," he hisses, standing beside me.

A warm sensation of pride twitches inside me as I see his look of discontent, as he looks me over. His blue eyes run over my dress, to my feet, then to the crown on my head, and back to my eyes. There is anger in his eyes, and I relish in it.

"Good evening, Prince Frąviné," I say, pretending not to notice, as I turn back to the guests.

"This is not the dress I requested. This dress is black."

The lace of my dress is covered with tiny black beads that

shimmer in the yellow lights from the chandeliers overhead. The sleeves of the dress come to my wrists, and neckline is a deep triangle shape, plunging far into my chest, but that is not where the lace ends; the lace comes all the way to my throat, stopping only halfway up my neck.

I see now why he had asked for me to wear a blue dress; his suit would have been the same colour. We would have matched, had I worn the shade of blue he had demanded. It would have been clear that he and I were a couple – it also would have been clear to the guests who would rule over them if the prince proposed to me.

How glad I am that I wore black.

"So it is," I settle, keeping my voice even.

Just then, Prince Novaåke and a young man with golden curls walk by. They slow their pace briefly as they pass us on the staircase. Prince Novaåke is watching me carefully, and I him. There is something in his expression that I do not recognise.

"This is a new dress," Prince Fṛaviné sneers, his face close enough to mine that I can feel the warm air from his lips on my cheek when he speaks. Clearly, he does not care that his brother may hear him speak to me this way. "You must have gone to the dressmaker's today. Why buy a black one, when I specifically asked for a blue one?"

Prince Novaåke and his companion continue down the stairs, though, I know that they are deliberately walking slowly; Prince Novaåke must be listening to our conversation.

"I liked this dress when I saw it on the rack," I say. "I thought it suited me."

"You lie."

"But why would I lie? I like this dress," I continue, now turning my hips from side to side for Prince Fṛaviné to see the layers of the skirt swish. "Don't you like it? Don't you think it suits me?"

"It's not the dress I asked you to wear."

"You mean, the dress you *ordered* me to wear?" I argue.

"Excuse me?"

"You can make your orders, Prince Fr*ą*viné, but I—"

He cuts me off through gritted teeth, "You do as I say! This is *my* kingdom!"

The prince now has me by the sleeve. His grip is firm and tight against me, his knuckles balled up in my black lace. There's a fire in his eyes that makes my chest flutter with fear, but I push it to the side for now. Now is not the time for fear; it is time for action.

Prince Fr*ą*viné wants a woman who will follow his commands, someone who will dress the way he wishes, and heed his every warning. He will not want someone defiant. Not like me.

Now, for the first time, since he stood next to me on the stairs, I look Prince Fr*ą*viné in the eyes. It's like a challenge. His expression is seething, and I am calm. I lean into him, our eyes locked as I inch nearer. I am deliberate and careful in my actions, near enough to him I feel the heat of his skin, though we do not touch.

"I do as I wish." My tone is deep and muted, practically a whisper. But it is steady and defiant. Stubborn and strong. Unmoving.

"Not for long," he mutters.

His face is an inch from mine, and I can practically feel the anger radiating off of his body. But he doesn't scare me. In fact, I lean in closer to him.

I whisper, "You may have this whole island scared shitless

of you, Price Frąvine, but I do not scare that easily."

He doesn't say anything to that.

With one last look of disappointment, Price Frąviné releases my arm, and storms back up the stairs. He stomps up the stone hallway, and I wait until I cannot hear his footsteps anymore, before I allow myself to release a shaking breath, which I had not known I'd been holding.

Then, when I am calm again, I continue down the staircase. I tip up the last of my first glass of champagne and place it on a passing silver tray.

Now the party can really begin.

It's nearly an hour later, and I've lost count after six flutes of champagne. Tonight, I have danced with no men; I've spoken to a couple of lords, who were friendly, but only out of obligation. I've palmed them off to the nearest woman, hoping that they will leave me alone – it's worked, for the most part.

I'm standing at the chocolate fountain, sipping my champagne, when a red blur makes its way onto the middle of the dance floor. When I blink again, I recognise the red dress. It's velvet and short, cut up the centre of the thigh, with a lower neckline and black lace on every edge.

And who could be wearing a red, velvet dress to a black and white themed ball? I must find out.

Fuelled by both excitement and alcohol, I beeline for the woman in the red dress. As I approach, it becomes increasingly obvious who would wear this dress. None other than…

"Lady Pénquil," I greet.

"Princess."

"I'm sure you misread the invitation."

She grins at me, those emerald eyes shining brightly.

Already, she's holding a flute of champagne. Most of her blonde hair is tied back in a loose bun, but symmetrical whisps on either side of her eyes hang to her chin. She looks even more beautiful than usual.

"Did I?" She smirks. "Is that why I feel so out of place?"

"Perhaps," I say with a shrug off my shoulders. "Or, perhaps, it's because you weren't with me."

I shock myself with my boldness. It is so unlike me to say something so outrageously daring, especially in front of so many people – especially to a woman.

Lady Pénquil, on the other hand, doesn't appear shocked; she looks charmed, in fact. Maybe impressed. Her face is no longer a sly grin, but rather a sincere smile. She considers me for a second, and I wait nervously.

"You are right." She holds out a hand to me, and I take it. "I should be by your side."

For the first twenty to thirty minutes, we pace around the ballroom, together. We greet guests, and Lady Pénquil introduces me to several of her Whŷstelkinér friends. We end up sharing a drink with the owner of the bakery; we laugh with bartenders from the tavern; we chat to various merchants and fishermen. Even though I am a thousand miles from home, this all feels so natural.

Then we dance. Lady Pénquil assumes the male role, taking my side in one hand and flittering me around the dancefloor. She twirls me, catches me, and holds me as we dance together, tipsy with the swelling warmth of alcohol in my belly.

My head feels fuzzy as the third dance ends. Looking in her eyes, I ask her, "Wanna go for a walk?"

"Love to."

Leaving my half-finished flute of champagne on a silver

tray, I lead her up by the hand. We walk together, fingers intertwined, up the stairs, and down a hallway. As I open a door to the garden, a cool wind brushes through me. Cool on my face, it pulls my hair and my dress, dragging them both into the air, filling my lungs with salt.

"Where are we going?" she asks.

"The garden," I whisper to her gently. Then I take her hand again and lead her onto the grass.

It's dark outside. The only light in the garden comes from the windows to the ballroom. It's quiet too. The music from inside is muted when I close to the door, leaving us in the soft dimness of the rose garden.

We sit on the grass, beside a tall tree that twinkles with lights. She's so close that I can feel the warmth from her body against me. I look at her closely, watching as I wait for something to happen.

"I had fun tonight," I whisper.

In the darkness of the garden, her green eyes peer into mine and I feel my stomach tickle again with excitement. Deliberately, Lady Pénquil lifts her hand to my face, her fingertips brushing my cheek. She's looking at me like she's never seen anything like me before. Like I'm an alien.

"What?" I whisper.

"You're beautiful."

She leans in slightly, and her thin lips brush mine.

When I withdraw from her, she looks startled, as though she expected us to stay like that forever.

"You are a strange type of woman," I tell her frankly.

She raises an eyebrow.

"How so?"

"You are woman who sometimes dresses like a man," I

begin to list. "A woman who kisses other women. Who makes other women feel… wonderful."

At first, she looks confused, but as I talk more, her face softens into a flirty grin. I watch her as she watches me closely. Her eyes flick over me, looking me up and down as she inches closer to me again, her cold hand on my side. She's so close that her lips graze my neck as she speaks.

"You feel wonderful, do you?" she purrs.

"Yes."

"Wonderful how?"

I feel embarrassment singe my cheeks. I am too nervous to look at her face. As I look down at the grass below, I gesture awkwardly to my lower stomach.

"Oh." There's a smile in her voice. "Well, I'm glad."

Lady Pénquil is looking at me again. Her intense green eyes watch mine. Her lips are slightly parted, a slither of straight teeth showing behind those thin, pink lips. As she stares at me, I feel myself growing more and more nervous. Is she seeing something abnormal? Is she seeing something displeasing?

Apparently not, because her mouth is on mine again, this time not as gentle. Kind of hungry and desperate. She kisses me so deeply that I feel her warm tongue in my mouth. And this time I don't let her kiss me; I kiss her back.

Her mouth tastes like champagne – but there's a sweetness behind it. A taste I don't recognise. Somehow, the taste of her tongue is like the smell of her skin.

Her hands are soft on my neck, her cold fingertips stroking my skin. I can hear her breathing as we kiss. It's not a soft breath, but harsh and tepid against my face. Her fingers are gentle at my throat. Her palms gently rest against my chest, fingertips cold on my skin.

She leans back from me for a second, her green eyes looking into mine. She pauses, eye-contact unbreaking, before she slides her hands down my body and rests them on my hips, grasping my sides firmly through the linen of my black dress. Something about the way she grabs me causes a gasp to ripple through me, pleasure seeping into my skin.

Suddenly, she's sitting on my lap, her legs on either side of my hips and her stomach pressed firm against mine. The velvet red dress hikes up her legs, revealing more thigh than I have ever seen on another person. Her upper legs are white as the moon shining in the night sky.

Unsure what else to do with my hands, I place them on her exposed upper legs. My thumbs instinctively begin to stroke her thighs, the soft skin tender against me.

Then, a bright light assaults my eyes. The suddenness of it rips Lady Pénquil and I apart. I look to the source of the light, lifting an arm to use as a visor against the unexpected brightness, squinting to see where the light could have come from.

"You see, Your Highness?" The first voice is unfamiliar.

"Yes, I see. Thank you, Servant. You may return to your duties." The second voice, however, I know all too well. "My princess, what exactly are you doing?"

I must take a breath to keep from growling at him. "What I please."

It is not shame that aches in my body. It is not embarrassment or guilt. It is irritation. It is anger. It is rage. Not only by the fact that we are interrupted, but also by the tone that Prince Frąviné uses when he speaks to me; as though what I have done is something to be ashamed of. As though he is disgraced by me.

"And with… who is this anyway?" Prince Frąviné turns the

lantern so that it is pointed at Lady Pénquil, who is still perched upon my lap. "What's your name, Miss?"

With a noise of discomfort at the light in her eyes, Lady Pénquil says, "Pénquil, the dressmaker."

"A dressmaker. A merchant, my princess." Prince Fraviné tuts disapprovingly. "How could you?"

"Lady Pénquil happens to be a—"

"*Lady?*" The prince chortles. He laughs heartily, as though I have made a joke. "This is nothing of the sort. Did you not hear her, Princess? She is a merchant! She is a dressmaker. She is of no status, at all."

I look at Pénquil, who is now staring down at her lap. Her shoulders have slumped, and her golden hair falls in curtains around her face.

"Well, why would I care about that, anyway?" I argue. "I'm not a superficial elitist, like you! Status might be important to you, but it isn't to me!"

"Enough of this!" the prince growls at me through gritted teeth.

He grabs Pénquil by the shoulder and reefs her from my lap, causing a cry of shock out of her. He drags her up so that she stands beside him on the grass, his face so close to hers that I almost think he's going to bite her.

"Let her go!" I demand, getting to my feet as well.

"You know, I don't think I will," Prince Fraviné snarls. Then he calls to a servant, who scurries over obediently. "Take this merchant to the dungeons."

He tosses Pénquil in the direction of the servant. She stumbles slightly, probably due to intoxication, while the servant grabs her by the wrist. By comparison, this tiny servant does not appear strong enough to drag Pénquil all the way to the dungeons – wherever they are – but he surprises me with his strength as he pulls her across the grass.

I start towards them, deciding that this will not happen – but the prince then has me by the sleeve of my dress again. He holds my arm in his fist, his hand comparably huge against mine. We stare at each other for a second. My pulse throbs in my throat. My head swims. I focus to steady my breaths.

"Let me go!" I command.

"Watch your tone," he whispers." He looks me up and down, his eyes flicking over my body with such sickening desire that my stomach curls. "You wouldn't believe the things I've done to get what I want."

"I know exactly what you've done," I spit at him. "I've read the letters."

The prince's face changes. His eyes are wide, his eyebrows furrowed. A muscle twitches in the prince's jaw. His grip on my wrist tightens. My fingers are going numb. Then, his piercing gaze moves from my eyes to the tiara that sits amongst the braids of my hair. Vengeance flashes across his features as he grabs it from my head, ripping out a few strands of hair as he does so.

"Don't!" I scream, fighting him.

I watch, helplessly, as he throws my mother's diadem into the grass, feeling my heart quivering in my chest.

"How dare you!" I try to wriggle out of his grasp, but he is far stronger than me.

At that moment, several more servants appear. Some, like Justrikk, I know from staying in the castle. I try to call out to them, but Prince Fraviné shoves me to the ground. My knees scrape along the grass, causing me to cry out in pain.

"Take this one, too, while you're at it," he commands the servants.

"Your Royal Highness," Justrikk says quietly, taking a step towards the prince, his arms outstretched in front of him as though to protect himself. "Prince Fraviné, are you sure? What about King Kelriaq? What will he say?"

"Take them to the dungeons, or you can go as well."

The threat is enough for Justrikk to wrap his hands around one of my elbows and pull me to my feet. He steers me out of the garden. When I fight back, another servant grabs my other elbow. Now they're basically carrying me, while I shout and kick out at both, demanding that they let me go.

"My father will hear about this!" I'm yelling at them.

Justrikk apologises under his breath as he and the other servants walk Pénquil and I around the side of the castle and down some stone stairs that I had never noticed.

"Let me go!" I shout.

The stairs lead into some sort of tunnel made of stone. It's cold down there, and dark. There's the sound of dripping water echoing throughout the stone tunnel. The way the sound ricochets off the walls makes it impossible to tell where the noise could be coming from.

When my eyes adjust to the darkness of the tunnel, I see that there are cells on either side of the stone hallway, iron bars separating each prisoner – although, there doesn't appear to be a soul trapped in this prison. Apart from us.

Despite my thrashing and hysterical screaming, Justrikk and the other servant are careful when they place me on the stone floor. Although their prince treats me as a traitor by locking me away, his servants remember that I am still a princess.

"I'm sorry, Princess Aruniar," Justrikk mumbles again, as he closes the iron-barred gate to my cell. "I'll tell Hazel that you're here."

"Tell my father!" I shout at him.

And then he's gone.

Chapter 19

As I sit in the dark, barely able to see the outline of Pénquil's body, I feel helplessness start to fill me up from the inside. It starts as numbness in my toes, and ends with a raging fire, burning the insides of my rib cage. Tears sting my eyes.
How could this happen?
This is all so sudden. Only a few days ago, I was trying to seduce Prince Frąviné, and now he's locking me away in a dungeon?
My first thought, after I wipe away my tears, is: I could try to escape. Hope glints and fades away, disappearing like a fleeting light at the far end of this stone tunnel. It seems useless to even try.
My second thought is more like a vision, a memory I thought I had forgotten. Screaming. Sweat. Ragged breathing. Crying. Blood. My mother's face.
The last time I felt this hopeless and alone.
The day my mother died.
I was there, all but fifteen, standing beside my mother in her bed chambers, when she was in labour. She gripped my arm at the elbow, her sweat-soaked face buried in my armpit. Her breaths were ragged and deep, panting rapidly into my loose-fitting dress. My mother's dark brown eyes looked into mine with fear and hopelessness. I had no idea that a single look on someone's face could shake me to my bones.
"Just get it out of me," my mother panted. Her voice was

desperate and afraid, shaking with anxiety. "Please."

Outside the castle, a storm was howling. The wind whistled loudly against the walls, heavy drops of rain spattering as hard as rocks on every window. While bolts of lightning flashed in the black sky, illuminating the courtyard for a split second, before the world returned to a fearsome, eerie blackness. The heavy sound of hail smashing against the roof disturbed not only me, but all who resided in the castle. The stunning kingdom hadn't seen a storm like this in decades.

"We're trying!" The doctor was no help. He had been standing at the end of the bed, yelling instructions at my mother as though she were a servant for hours. "Push harder!"

"Stop yelling at her!" I had shouted at the doctor. "Can't you see my mother is in pain?"

Despite only being fifteen, I was bold. My mother had always said that I had courage beyond my years, and today was no different. I was not about to let some man shout at the Queen of Nashwalte, not in front of me. She had been pushing for hours. She was exhausted. She was in pain.

"It's okay, Aruniar," my mother told me. She rubbed my arm, panting breathlessly.

Queen Elora, my mother, groaned and yelled in pain. The screaming hurt my ears. She made sounds that I had only heard in my nightmares.

"Where is my husband?" she breathed to a nearby servant.

"He's not here, Your Majesty," the servant told her gently.

"Get him!"

"He's out, Your Majesty. Please understand. You have to do this without him."

"You have to keep pushing, Your Majesty." Another servant, an older lady, my mother's handmaiden, came over to my mother, dabbing her forehead with a wet cloth. "Soon, there will be a beautiful baby. All you have to do is push."

Hot tears slipped down my mother's cheeks. She pushed her face further into my armpit, groaning ever louder, her whole-body contorting as she strained to birth my baby brother.

And then I noticed the blood.

"Gods. Queen Elora, stop pushing!" There was panic in the doctor's voice. I remember him looking from me to the servants with panic, and then he pointed to the younger servant. "Get towels! Now!"

"What have you done to her?" I shouted at the doctor. "What did you do?"

"Get her out of here," the doctor told the other servant.

"No!" I wrestled against the servant, who tried to grab my wrists. I clung to my mother, gripping her arms, so that I couldn't be dragged away from her. "I won't leave her!"

"Princess, come on," the servant said to me, trying to pry my hands from the queen. "Be reasonable."

"Aruniar." My mother's voice was quiet, raspy. Her breaths were shallow and groaning. "Aruniar."

"I'm not leaving you!" By now, tears burned my eyes, wet my cheeks and swelled my throat. My voice was a desperate cry, like that of a toddler.

Just then, my mother's handmaiden, looking dishevelled and frightened out of her wits, returned to the bed chamber, carrying armfuls of towels. She crouched at the foot of the bed; beside the doctor whose face looked stricken.

Blood, dark and red, was seeping into the mattress, a wide circle of blood widening around my mother's body. The puddle of blood smelled of iron, twisting an uncomfortable lump inside my stomach.

"Doctor," the handmaiden urged, her voice low. She huddled close to the doctor, whispering, "What do we do now?"

"She's lost too much blood," the doctor said in a hushed voice. Perhaps he thought I couldn't hear.

My mother was starting to twitch, the colour draining from her face. Her breaths were becoming slow and wheezy, sounding as though she was sleeping. She didn't make any noises of pain now; just wheezing breaths, fighting for oxygen.

"Do something!" I shouted at the doctor. "She'll bleed out!"

"Get her out of here," the doctor told mother's lady-in-waiting, who looked pale and sick as she stood useless in the corner. "Hurry up."

I remember a servant touching my shoulder. I remember them standing in front of me, trying to encourage me to leave. I remember shoving them when they tried to take my hand.

"Your Highness," the servant pleaded. "Come with me. You can't be here."

"I'm not leaving my mother!"

The towels were useless. All they did was soak up my mother's blood. There were at least a half dozen of them, piled at the foot of the bed, all of them soaked in blood.

Coming back to my reality, where I I sit alone in the dark prison, my third thought is: what would my mother say if she saw me now? Would she understand why I'm here? Would she be angry with me for being with a woman? Would that even matter to her?

Chapter 20

It's impossible to tell night from day in the prison. In a tunnel this deep in the ground, no sunlight could hope to penetrate the dungeons. Consequently, I have no idea how long we have been down here.

I had tried shouting for help. I had tried for… well, judging by my parched throat and aching voice, it had been hours of screaming and shouting. Trying to get someone's attention, despite knowing that it was no use. If sunlight couldn't breach the walls of this prison, a mortal's voice wouldn't either.

In the cell beside mine, separated by rusted iron bars, Pénquil is curled up in a ball in the corner. Her red velvet dress, which had once been captivating and alluring, was now plastered in dirt and grime from the dirty floors of the prison cell.

"Pénquil," I had tried to comfort through the bars, probably hours ago now. "It's going to be okay. I'll get us out."

She had not said a word since Prince Fraviné had ordered our imprisonment. She had not spoken a word to me since he had caught us in the rose garden. Perhaps she was ashamed that she had tricked me; perhaps she felt guilty for lying to me about her name – but I did not care for titles. If I had, I probably would have agreed to marry Prince Fraviné by now.

"Pénquil," I try again, creeping close to the iron bars between us, reaching my arm through the bars to try to reach her. "Are you okay? Do you want to talk?"

Silence.

"Pénquil, please. I'm not angry with you. Please talk to me."
Still nothing.

She's on the opposite side of the cell, facing away from me. Her body looks so small curled up against the back of the cell, and so far, away. I want nothing more than to be able to touch her, hold her, kiss her – but she won't even acknowledge that I am here.

Pretty soon after that, I fall asleep.

I do not know how long I sleep for, or how long I am awake for after that. I do not know whether it has been hours, days or weeks. Time is meaningless. After some time, there is the sound of footsteps coming down the hallway, and a dim yellow light that sways with a walking body.

It is Prince Frąviné. He stands on the other side of the bars, looking down at me.

"Well, you've had two days to come to your senses," the prince tells me, his voice sweet as it echoes in the dungeons. "Are you ready to apologise to me, Aruniar?"

"It's *Princess* Aruniar to you," I correct him.

"That's a no, I take it."

"I have nothing to apologise for."

The prince scoffs. "You left my ball to fraternise with a merchant! You think that that is nothing of my concern?"

I shrug. "It doesn't involve you, does it?"

"Except that you are my betrothed."

"You did not ask me to marry you," I argue.

"I asked your father."

My eyes shoot to his. There's a wicked smile on Prince Frąviné's face as he looked down at me, blue eyes practically sparkling in the light of his lantern. In this light, the tiny fire flickering inside the lantern, surrounded by darkness, I see the prince for what he truly is. Eéijrwãrmpạs is not the monster that haunts this island; it is Frạviné.

"You didn't know?" He snickers.

"My father knows how I feel about you."

"And yet, he approved of our engagement."

How like him, to not ask a woman for her consent before deciding her fate, for his own personal gain.

A bitter taste tingles on my tongue. I suddenly feel sick. The world spins around me and I wonder whether I'm going to throw up. My father approved my engagement, without asking me.

Why is he so set on me marrying Prince Frạviné of all men?

"We are still engaged to be married," the prince tells me smoothly, continuing in a casual tone. "And I would still like to marry you, Princess Aruniar – but only if you do as I say. If you repent what you've done."

"I will not."

"Are you sure about that?"

"Certain."

"Then mark my words, Aruniar, you will rot in these dungeons!" His casual tone is gone now, replaced only by a thundering shout of red-hot anger.

"Fine."

Then he storms out, taking his lantern with him, leaving Pénquil and I alone in the dark again.

"Pénquil!" I call to her once I am sure that the prince is gone. "Are you awake? I want to talk to you. Please speak to me."

Silence.

The next time we have a visitor is after I have slept again. It is Hazel. She stands on the other side of the bars, her eyes wet with tears and her mouth a worried line of pure gloom.

"Princess," she sighs sadly. "How did this happen?"

"It was Prince Fṛaviné," I tell her.

"What did that snake do to you?"

"He found Pénquil and I in the garden during the black and white ball. Justṛikk, and some others, locked us in here. You must tell my father where I am!"

Hazel freezes. She looks at me carefully from the other side of the bars, confusion clear on her face. "You and Pénquil, the dressmaker?"

"Yes."

"In the garden?"

"Yes."

"At night?"

"Yes, Hazel!" My voice comes out in a huff of frustration and irritability. "I was with Pénquil, the dressmaker. We were in the garden at night, *kissing*, okay?"

"Oh, princess." She shakes her head disapprovingly, and I feel even angrier than before. "What would the king say?"

"The king doesn't even know I'm down here!" I shout. "Tell him what happened, and tell him that I'm here! Tell him that we are going home the second Pénquil and I get out of this prison!"

"King Kelriaq is occupied," Hazel replies evenly.

"What?"

"The king is busy. He cannot come."

"What is more important that his daughter being trapped in a prison?" I demand.

"I cannot say."

"Excuse me?"

"Princess, please understand," Hazel says, trying to soothe me. "Your father cannot come to your aid now. He is quite busy.

Do you have a plan for getting out, perhaps?"

A fair question, to which I do not have any answer yet.

"Here, eat this."

My maid holds out a bread roll to me, passing it through the bars. Her hands are too big to fit between the bars, but the roll from the bakery slips through easily, landing in my hands.

"I am not hungry," I say stubbornly.

"Your Highness, you have been here for four days," Hazel argues crossly. "You must be hungry. Please eat."

"Do you have food for Pénquil?"

"No."

"Then I will not eat," I decide.

"Princess!"

"Hazel, I will not eat this unless there is enough for Pénquil as well," I resolve, now feeling a sudden calm wash over me. "I will not let her wither away to nothing, while I eat enough to sustain me."

"Why must you make everything so difficult?" Hazel snaps, throwing her hands up in the air. "Fine. I will be back shortly, with more bread. Please, in the meantime, just eat this."

She stomps down the echoey stone hallway and disappears.

When I yawn and open my eyes, apparently having fallen asleep, Hazel is standing outside my cell, holding an armful of bread. She passes it through the bars to me, and I pile it onto the skirt of my dress to keep it from touching the concrete floor.

"Happy?" Hazel questions.

"Extremely. Now go tell my father that I'm here."

"I cannot."

"Why not?"

"Your Highness, the king is… he is ill."

I feel my stomach twist into a tight knot. It swirls disturbingly, and if there were anything in my stomach, I would probably be sick.

"My father is ill?" I repeat.

"Yes," Hazel breathes. "He has been asking for you."

"And what have you told him?" I demand. "Nothing? You haven't told him where I am or what happened to me?"

"This is why I didn't want you to know."

"Why?"

"Your Highness," Hazel says slowly, softly. "Your father... he may die."

"Surely... surely you know a remedy for his ailment," I stammer, forcing the words out of my mouth. "Surely you can make him a tea or a... a medicine that will cure him of his ailment."

"I cannot."

"Why?"

"I have never seen an illness quite like this, Your Highness."

"Let me out of this cell, now!" I shout.

"I don't have a key—"

"Then get one!"

"Princess Aruniar," Hazel says softly. "I understand that you are angry. I would be angry too."

"You have no idea what I feel!" I scream at her. "Get me out of here!"

"I can't!"

"Then, get out!"

"Princess—"

"Go!"

And she does. Then, it's just Pénquil and I alone in the prison, again. I imagine that Pénquil must be feeling some guilt for giving me the silent treatment, as she now turns to look at me from her cell. Her eyes are red, as though she's been crying, and there are dark circles around them. They look sunken and exhausted. I wonder if she has slept.

"Are you okay?" she asks me. Her voice is husky, perhaps from crying, or maybe from not speaking in days. "You must be sad."

"I'm angry," I whisper, turning to the floor.

Pénquil scoots across the stone and comes to sit at the bars that separate us. She reaches her hand through the bars and touches me gently on the shoulder. Although we cannot embrace, I am grateful that she is there. Her company is enough.

"I'm sorry about your father."

"Me too."

We talk for a while, then I hand her some bread. We talk a little more, and then we both fall asleep, heads resting against the iron bars – almost touching.

"Princess?" It's Pénquil whispering to me from her side of the iron bars. "Princess Aruniar, are you awake?"

Blinking awake, I rub my eyes with my knuckles. It's still just as dark down here as before. It's still impossible to tell whether it's night or day; the sound of dripping water still echoes off the stone walls of the tunnel; I'm still trapped in a cage like a pet rat.

"You can drop the 'princess'," I tell her in a hushed voice, looking down at the stone floor beneath me. "Princesses don't get locked in dungeons. I'm just Aruniar now."

She is quiet for a minute or so. In the silence between us, I can practically hear her thinking, mulling this over. Her presence is warm and comforting beside me. Even though we've barely talked since we were thrown in here, I am grateful for her company. Without her to keep me stable, I might have gone insane in the darkness of this tunnel, alone and helpless, with nothing to fight for. Nothing to live for.

For a moment, I wonder whether she has had these same feelings that I have had.

Has she been feeling as secluded and terrified as I have these past few days?

"Aruniar." Her voice is easy and soothing. The tender tone she uses reminds me of the way one might address a young child who has lost their parents in a busy marketplace. "You have such a pretty name."

That surprises me. That is not what I had expected her to say.

"Thank you."

In the dimness of the shadowy tunnel, the only part of Pénquil I can make out is the blurry outline of her face, the golden shade of her hair. I briefly recall her hair being in a loose bun the last time I saw her in decent lighting, but now, it seems to hang loosely around her shoulders, grimy and matted.

"Think we'll ever get out of here?" she asks me with a sigh, leaning her back against the bars.

I weigh the options in my mind. I could tell her the truth: that as long Prince Frąviné has any power, we will likely die down here. Or, I could lie to make her feel better, to let her keep some of that hope that lingers vaguely in her voice. As much as I appreciate holding on to the tiny whisps of optimism that dangle between us, I know that I can't fib to the woman I... care for.

"Probably not."

After a few seconds of quiet, Pénquil says, in a voice as dry as sand, "Hmm, well, that's unfortunate."

I can't help the little smile that creeps onto my lips. Even in the face of a fate as grim as death by starvation and dehydration, Pénquil, the merchant, still has her improbable witticism. Even at a time as tense and chilling as this, I find myself attracted to her. Her wit, her absurdity, her charm.

"Tell me again about your home." In the dark cell beside mine, I hear Pénquil turn her body around to face me, holding onto the bars to steady herself.

"My country is mostly rainforest," I tell her vaguely.

Suddenly, I'm there, standing in my bed chambers back home in Nashwalte. Outside my window, birds call from the deep forests. Their whistles and songs reverberate through the trees, a familiar melody that I know all too well. Trees taller, wider than any building, rustle vociferously in the warm breeze. The scent in the air is not salty like Whŷstelkiné, but damp wood and vibrant green leaves.

"Are there animals?"

"Yes, but they don't come close to Willcrest. Unless they are pets," I explain, thinking of my sleepy housecat, Jipperiya. She has probably spent most of my time away sleeping in my bed chambers. "I haven't seen any larger animals here."

"There are animals here," Pénquil corrects me. "They live in the mountains."

"What kind of animals?"

"Just wolves," she describes. "You have to make sure that you build a fire before dark, so that you can see them coming at night."

"That sounds scary," I say.

"Only if you're alone."

"What else is in the mountains?"

"Not much." Pénquil seems to think to herself for a long moment, seeming to decide whether she will share all that she knows, before she adds, "People live out there."

"They must be crazy to live so close to the wolves."

"They're not afraid of them," she says confidently in the dark.

"Why would anyone choose to live out there, so far away from society?"

"That's why they did it. To get away from society."

"Why would they do that?"

There's a tinge of accusation in Pénquil's voice when she says, "Aruniar, not everybody loves the monarchy."

"Yeah, well," I sigh. "Neither do I right now."

"For what it's worth, I told you Prince Frąviné was a bad guy."

"I *really* don't need an 'I told you so' right now."

Pénquil chuckles friskily on her side of the iron bars. I feel her cold hand reach through the bars and graze my scalp, caressing the back of my head.

"Sorry," she offers. "I was just kidding."

Again, I'm impressed by her ability to make a joke, during everything, in the uneasiness of this ghastly, frosty, murky prison cell. Somehow, she can see the funny side. That's the thing that I find most alluring about her right now, as I feel the urge to kiss her tear at my insides.

Chapter 21

By now, I've gotten used to the coolness of the tunnel. The way the frosty air settles into my skin and rattles my body so deep that it clatters inside my bones no longer alarms me; in fact, there's even a serenity to this coldness, a comfort to the pain of icy darkness.

Perhaps this is what it feels like when Delrossa takes you.

Is this the Heavens? How long have we been locked up here?

It's impossible to tell, in terms of days or weeks, but I know that we have run out of bread to share by the time Prince Frąviné visits next, a smirk on his face as usual.

Pénquil and I had been talking about the rainforests back home when we heard his footsteps on the stone floor. We had both silenced when he approached, Pénquil curling back into a ball and I standing at the gate.

"What do you want?" I sneer at him.

"So, I hear someone let you know about King Kelriaq," Prince Frąviné says proudly.

"Yeah, so?"

"So, do you want him to live, Aruniar?"

"What?"

"Do you want him to live?"

I stare at him blankly in the dim light of the lantern he holds in his hand. The candlelight flickers dully, casting yellow splashes of light on the stone walls and floor. Somehow, Prince Frąviné appears bigger in the darkness.

"Because, if you do, I recommend that you apologise to me, for your deceit and your filthy adultery."

I snort. "Adultery? Really?"

"Your unchastity is an uncouth insult to our betrothal!" Prince Frąviné scowls at me through the iron bars.

"Unchastity?" I repeat.

This doesn't stop the prince from yelling at me, or accusing me of things that I, in fact, have not done. He continues, "Lying with a woman when you are engaged to a man. A prince, no less! How could you do this?"

I do not argue the fact that we did not sleep together; it is irrelevant, and to dispute him over this matter would be pointless. Less than pointless. Trying to convince Prince Frąviné to release us would be in vain.

So, I say nothing. Despite the light from his lantern being harsh on my eyes, I simply stare at him, daring him to ask for my apology again.

"Very well," Prince Frąviné says nonchalantly, looking me up and down before he turns away from me. "If you've made your choice, then I guess I can't persuade you to change your mind, can I?"

I don't speak. At first, the prince seems to wait patiently. As the duration of the silence grows, Prince Frąviné seems to become more and more irritated. When he finally turns back to look me in the eyes, I see the blueness in his eyes giving way to a raging fire.

"Fine then," he growls. "Rot down here."

Then he is gone. He takes his lantern and all the light from the tunnel with him, as he plods through the dark, vanishing after quite some time.

"Seems like he wants you to say you're sorry," Pénquil says

to me in a whisper when we're both sure that he's gone.

"You think?"

"Well, maybe you should."

"Are you out of your mind?" I exclaim, my voice echoing in the stone prison. "Why would I apologise? I did nothing wrong, and neither did you!"

"I know that, *Aruniar*!" I am taken aback by the way she says my name; it's as though it is an insult. She takes a deep breath and calmly adds, "I mean, maybe you could trick him."

The next time Prince Fraviné walks up the tunnel, I have a plan. It is immoral. It is a wicked thing to do, this plan, but it may be our only hope of getting out of this prison alive.

"How are you not dead yet?" is his greeting.

As if on cue, my stomach rumbles. It twists ravenously. Perhaps I have gotten to the point of starvation that I no longer notice my hunger, or perhaps I am simply too close to death for sustenance to feel so imperative.

"So, what's it going to be, Aruniar?" the prince asks me. There's a bizarre and uncanny sort of calm that seems to occupy Prince Fraviné in this moment.

It gives me an idea.

"Prince Fraviné, please." For these three words, I put on the falsest of voices, a tone so meek and remorseful that I almost cringe at the sound of my own voice. "Forgive me."

My mother did not raise me this way. She raised me to stand up to injustice, to face every undue action with courage and confidence. She would not stand for this falsity, this falsehood of apology. But my mother is not here, and I am on the brink of death, at the hands of a vile man who would rather see me dead than consider his own actions.

"For?" the Prince of Whŷstelkiné presses.

"For my adultery," I express, using the same words that he had. "My unfaithfulness to you... and my country."

"You wronged me."

"You are right. I shouldn't have slept with La... with Pénquil." I use that dishonest, submissive voice to plead with him. "It was wrong, and I regret it. Please forgive me."

Prince Frąviné considers me for a long moment, his piercing blue eyes drilling into me in the light of the lantern he holds in his hand. He's thinking as he looks me over. His sturdy gaze is forceful and concentrated, as though there is nothing in existence, apart from the two of us. It is disturbing, in a painful sort of way.

"All right," he grunts. "I'll forgive you, Aruniar."

"Thank you, Prince Frąviné!" I gasp, using my best a mock-appreciative tone. "When I marry you, you shall make kind and merciful rule—"

He interjects, "If..."

There's an if.

"You kill that filthy, slut of a merchant you insisted on being unfaithful to me with," he concludes, now turning his stare towards Pénquil, who shrinks timidly into her cell.

"Kill her?" I breathe.

"That's what I said. Kill her, and I'll forgive you. I'll release you, your father will be cured, and you will be my bride," the prince articulates, speaking leisurely and patently. "If you're truly sorry, you'll do this for me."

"To murder someone, Your Royal Highness, it's not so easy..."

"I disagree," Prince Frąviné contends. "I have found that killing is quite effortless, when one deserves it."

Did he just admit to murder?

I wonder how this information could assist us, how we could use this as evidence to gain an advantage. But who would believe us? Two women against the word of a man? A prince, no less?

"Your Royal Highness," I breathe. "Please understand. I don't have the heart to kill someone, especially someone that I regard as a friend."

The prince nods. "I do understand. I understand that you, Princess Aruniar of Nashwalte, are a liar."

"I'm not a liar," I claim.

"Then prove that you are remorseful. Prove that you regret your actions. Kill the merchant!"

When I turn to look at Pénquil, I see that she is watching me from her side of the iron bars. She does not appear afraid; the look in her eyes is stubborn and brave. Subtly, she nods. Only once. It's a tiny, almost imperceptible motion that I might have missed had I not been paying attention. It's an undisclosed action, shared only between us. She has a plan.

"Fine," I answer, getting to my feet, meeting Prince Fraviné's eye. "I'll kill her, if it means that you will forgive me."

The prince looks at me a few moments longer, as though he is deciding whether he believes me. Then, without a word, he steps forward, withdrawing a rusty key from his pocket and begins unlocking the iron bars that contains me. The key *clinks* loudly in the lock, and the gate swings open with a creaking whine.

I can hardly believe that my plan has worked—sort of—as I step out of the cell. I move gingerly, taking small steps, until I'm standing beside Prince Fraviné, who is still watching me carefully.

"All right, go on," he says. "Kill her."

"I need you to let her out of the cell first," I tell him.

"How do I know you won't escape?"

"Don't you trust me, my prince?"

An amused smile quirks his lip, his blue eyes flicking from my lips to my eyes.

It gives me an idea.

Thinking quickly, I swish my filthy black dress in his direction. I look up at the prince with an expression that I can only describe as seductive and take a step closer to him. It takes all the bravery I can muster to lean my body against his.

"What are you doing?" He is rigid in response to my touch, secure in his thoughts, not persuaded.

"What I should have done long ago," I whisper to him.

Leaning into his firm body, one hand flat on his chest, I plant a firm kiss on his lips. I wonder how good of an actor I am as I reach my hand into his.

Will he fall for this?

In one swift motion, I withdraw the lantern from his hand, swinging it behind my body and using the full force of my weight to smash the lantern against the side of the prince's face.

The glass and candle from the lantern fall with a *clatter* to the stone floor as Prince Fraviné lets out a sudden cry of agonising pain. In the sudden darkness, it's difficult to see, but I hear his feet as he stumbles backwards. In the few seconds that follow, I manage to snatch the key from his other hand, jamming it into the lock on Pénquil's cell.

Pénquil races to the gate of her cell as I struggle to turn the rusty key, my whole body shaking, my breaths quick as the cold air burns my chest.

"You're not getting away that easy!" Prince Fraviné shouts at me, grabbing my arm in the palm of his large hand.

"Let me go!" I scream at him, clawing at his hand.

Now in total dimness, with no candlelight, I can barely make out the prince's shape beside me. I try desperately to push him away from me, but he holds me securely in place, gripping me at my shoulder.

"You tried to trick me!" Prince Frąviné shrieks.

"Release me, you monster!"

While I struggle with the prince, clawing at his hand and pushing at his body, Pénquil reaches through the bars to turn the key in the lock. Keeping the prince's attention on me, I use both of my hands to shove Prince Frąviné away from me, my muscles aching with the struggle.

I lift my foot as high as I can and kick it into his stomach. The impact of the blow knocks me onto my back, bashing the wind out of me as I land with a hard *thud* on the stone floor. Then the gate unlocks and Pénquil pushes it open, she helps me up and we run.

Chapter 22

It feels as though we have been running forever. The icy air of the tunnel, combined with being winded from landing on my back when Prince Frąviné and I fought, causes my heart and chest to burn with desolation.

"We'll have to get back to the castle." I am barely able to catch my breath as we sprint through the tunnel. "I have to save my father."

"Aruniar, I don't think that's a good idea," Pénquil tells me.

"What? He's my father!"

"We can't risk Prince Frąviné catching us! He will kill us if he catches up with us. You must know that."

"He will kill my father if I don't save him!"

"We have the best chance of escaping if we go now. I will take you to the mountains," she explains. "We'll escape into the mountains, and no one will know where we've gone. We'll assume new identities. We'll live peacefully."

I stop to breathe. I pant wheezily, doubling over to take some deep gulps of air. The tunnel still feels cold on my skin, despite the tiny beads of sweat that gather around my hairline and drip at the side of my face.

"I know you're scared," Pénquil tells me. "I'm scared too."

In the smallest ray of sunshine that peaks through the tunnel, I see Pénquil's green eyes, their warmth, their sparkle. She looks at me with a tenderness that I don't recall ever seeing before.

Has anyone ever seen me as Pénquil sees me?

"We must keep going. He might catch us." Pénquil takes my hand and gives it a gentle tug, starting to jog again in the direction of the sunlight. "Come on."

As we reach the end of the tunnel, the sunlight blinding as we emerge from the mouth of the stone tunnel. In the light of the day, when my eyes adjust, I see the panic on Pénquil's face, but it is not enough to stop me. I shake my head, already deciding what I will do.

"I have to go back for my father," I insist.

"Aruniar, no!" she argues. "Please, just come with me. If he catches you, he will kill you – or maybe worse! I know somewhere safe we can go."

"I don't care," I resolve. "I will not let my father die at the hands of that vile prince!"

"He might be dead already!" Pénquil is looking at me with an expression that I believe to be pity. It stings to have her look at me this way, even more than her words. "How do you know he didn't already kill your father and pretend that he hadn't, just to get you to marry him?"

"I don't."

"Exactly. Now, come on."

Pénquil pulls again on my hand, but my feet a rooted to the ground where I stand. As I let my fingers slip from hers, I see now that we are a step apart. There's a pang in my chest. We stand a few steps away from each other, and there is space between our hands, where she has let me go.

She will leave me here. She will desert me.

Something like betrayal pricks the inside of my lungs. It burns from the inside, but I don't let it show on my face. I meet her eyes, keeping the emotion from creeping onto my expression as I try to appear composed, despite the tears that threaten behind my eyelids.

"I will not abandon hope," I decide. "I am going back for my father."

"Please, Aruniar! It is not safe!" She looks urgently over my shoulder, her face stricken with fear, her green eyes frantic with worry. "We're running out of time!"

"Fine," I tell her plainly. "Go without me."

"I cannot!"

"Don't then," I hiss. "Either way, I will save my father!"

Breaking into a run as I reach the rose garden, I leave Pénquil standing alone at the mouth of the tunnel.

I have left her before she managed to leave me.

Secretly, I hope that she will change her mind. I hope that she will wait for me, somewhere in the castle, while I tend to my father. I speak to Frewope the Devoted, asking her to allow me this one favour – let Pénquil wait for me.

As I enter the castle, stepping lightly so not to be noticed, I pray that she is wrong about my father, and that the three of us will be headed back to Nashwalte as soon as I get my father out of bed.

I will not abandon hope.

By the time I reach the West Wing, my breaths come in gasps again, from running. I had sprinted through the castle and up the stairs, avoiding the dining and sitting rooms, intending to only see my father. I will not be stopped.

Until I am stopped.

The door to my father's quarters opens, and Justrikk is there, beside another servant who holds a silver tray. The two whisper in quiet voices, huddling together by the door. Despite straining my ears to listen, I cannot hear their conversation from here.

Then I see Justrikk pat the other servant on the shoulder. The lord-in-waiting and I make eye-contact.

I know I am caught, so I step out from my hiding place as the other servant disappears, carrying the silver tray out of sight. Justrikk meets me in the centre of the hallway.

"Princess Aruniar," he breathes, his face tight and worried as he looks me over. "I believed you to be dead."

"Bet you wish I was," I say to him, my tone threatening. I size him up. I could probably take him; he's not quite as tall as me, and he's very slim, feeble even. "Lucky for you, I've got more important things to worry about."

"Your Highness!" Justrikk grabs my arm as I pass him.

"Unhand me," I command, brutally shrugging him off. "Who exactly do you think you are? Where is Hazel?"

"She's... He looks at me like how I imagine a deer looks at a mountain lion, frozen. "She's... well..."

"I need to see my father."

"Don't go in there."

"Why?"

"Your father... Your Highness, he is dead."

Terror pangs in my chest. My breaths come in shallow, ragged bursts. My vision blurs. My ears ring. The world spins around me. I feel tears spring to my tears, but I bravely stare Justrikk down, struggling to appear unconvinced.

"And why should I believe you?" I try to keep my voice even.

"Trust me. Please."

I side-step Justrikk and stride confidently towards my father's quarters. As I reach for the door handle, I hesitate, my fingers outstretched, as I consider the possibility that Justrikk is not lying to me.

"Please, listen," he says again, his voice low as he edges closer to me, moving deliberately, cautiously, as though I were an unpredictable wild animal. "King Kelriaq is dead. He was poisoned. There is nothing you can do. Please, just get out of here."

"I need to see for myself."

"No!"

As I open the door to my father's quarters, I feel Justrikk's hand on my arm, trying to pull me back. His hand is small against my own, and for a moment, I wonder how much force it would take to plunge him into the stone floor.

But then I am frozen in the doorway.

I feel despair seep into my skin.

My father.

He looks so minute and frail. He looks… not like himself at all. His skin, which once had been as brown as cocoa, is now a chilling shade of grey. His shoulders, once strong and wide, appear weak and bony against his sides. His body just lies on the bed, a pathetic mass of emptiness and insignificance.

And then I know.

I don't need to touch him. I don't need to feel for a pulse or to listen to his heartbeat. I just know.

Delrossa has taken him.

Kelriaq, the Brave King, is dead.

Chapter 23

"There is somewhere safe you can go," Justrikk is saying to me as he leads me by the hand, down the stairs and back towards the garden. "The mountains. They are south-east. Go through the crops. There are farmers who will not know you. Ask them about the mountains."

My head floats above me, wholly useless. Meaningless. The world is meaningless. Life is meaningless. It's all meaningless. All of this… it was for nothing.

I have lost everything.

And then it occurs to me: I am an orphan. Both of my parents are dead, taken by Delrossa the Merciful. My mother died a little over six years ago, trying to give me a baby brother; and my father, too, sometime in the last few days.

I have no family.

Everyone I have loved is dead.

I remember my mother lying in her bed chamber, a pool of blood around her body, her limp hand in mine. She lay there, as grey as a storm cloud, her face frozen in pain for all eternity. In her bed, she lay silent. Pulseless. Motionless. Lifeless.

It was days before the coroner was allowed to take her body. I remember my father at her bedside, grasping her hand with both of his, tears streaming down his face. It was the first, and last, time I ever saw my father cry. For days, King Kelriaq sat at my mother's bedside. He loved her so. I never expected that in my life I would find a love quite as magnificent as theirs, but I had always hoped.

I had been lurking at the doorway, concealed by the half-closed door to my mother's chambers, watching as the King of Nashwalte refused to have his wife taken to the cemetery, where Delrossa would take her back.

"You will not take her!" my father had shouted at the coroner.

"Your Majesty, please. She must be laid to rest." The coroner wore a black hood over his head, as all in our country do until their dead are buried. "It is time to let go."

"I will never let go!" The raw agony my father felt in his heart was evident on his despairing, tormented expression. The tears that soaked his cheeks were a testament to his pain. How I wished I could take it from him.

"What kind of afterlife do you imagine Elora having if she is not buried?"

"*Queen* Elora."

It is customary for Nashwaltian royalty to lose their titles once they have perished. My father knew this, but he acted as though he was blind to this fact. Up until his death, he still referred to my mother by her title: Queen Elora. Perhaps it was his way of grieving. Perhaps he held my mother in such high esteem that he simply couldn't see her as an ordinary woman.

Suddenly, I'm back in the rose garden. Justrikk is standing in front of me, his hands gripping my shoulders, his face close to mine. His words fall upon deaf ears; I see only his mouth moving as he speaks to me. The world is silent, as though I am suspended in water. The world moves in slow motion around me. I am a cloud, hanging loosely in the sky, not living a life, but observing one.

I feel his tight grip on my wrist as he drags me to the far side of the rose garden. His hand is warm around my forearm. He walks quickly, his stride a little too hasty for me to keep up with in such a daze.

When he releases my wrist, I am startled. Finally, I hear his voice when he speaks.

"Princess Aruniar, you must go!" Justrikk urges. "If His Royal Highness finds you here… there is no telling what he might do. You must get out of here!"

He gives me a push so that I am standing on the retaining wall that holds the rose garden, separating it from the flowering meadow below. Judging by the size of the blades of grass and daisies below, I'm assuming that the retaining wall can't be higher than I am tall.

"Your Highness! Go!"

"How far is it?"

"It's safe! You won't be hurt. Just go!"

With that, I take the jump off the retaining wall and land clumsily on my back in the grass below. My back aches, daisies and blades of grass impairing my vision as I lie face-up, looking up at the sky.

"Justrikk?" I groan, my voice hoarse as I cough a daisy out of my throat.

Nothing.

Perhaps he is gone.

It is utterly silent in the meadow. The soft rustling of the grass in the gentle wind is the only sound. Not a person or animal can be heard.

All of a sudden, I am painfully aware of how dreadfully alone I am. My father is dead. Hazel has deserted me. Pénquil has left me. I am all alone in a tired meadow, hiding from a prince whose only desire is to kill me with his bare hands.

Too winded to move, I let the pain wash over me, while I catch my breath. Greif and loneliness settle in my skin, they take turns filling me up with a cold anxiety that rattles me from within. I can do nothing but stare up at the clouds that drift lazily across the sky.

Night comes, and still I lie in the meadow, looking up at the stars that twinkle in the heavens high above me. The silky night sky gazes down upon me, and I find myself begging the gods that I make it through the night; that I manage to find the strength to stand and make my way to the villages in the south-east mountains.

And then, by the grace of the Goddess of Life herself, I do. With a deep breath of the cool night air, I get to my feet, brush myself off, and head south-east. My bare feet tingle numbly against the ground as I take steps away from the rose garden.

Under me, I feel dirt and small, loose rocks. Some stab the soles of my tender feet, and I make tiny sounds of pain as a rock or small stick scratches my skin. Perhaps, I should have brought shoes, or perhaps I should not complain. I barely escaped Whŷstelkiné with my life – in fact, there is still a chance that I may not!

Somewhere in the distance, hidden among tall blades of grass and white daisies, I hear crickets. Tiny night insects chirping and chittering to one another, warning more of their kinds that I am approaching, a giant in their midst. It reminds me of the sounds of the rainforest back home; cicadas and grasshoppers alike, chirruping at the sound of danger.

After a short while, guided by the light of the full moon, I come to a fence, a little taller than me, made of iron, not unlike the prison cell I was trapped in, save for the fact that these bars are cross-checked, welded together on each corner. The gaps in these iron bars are much too tiny for my hand to fit through, probably designed to keep out pests, but I can climb them.

I wedge my big toe into a gap in the rusty, squared iron fence. Holding the fence with hands to keep myself steady, I use all my strength to heave myself up on top. My body shakes with uneasiness as I sit upon the iron barrier, one leg on either side. To my left is the empty meadow of grass and daisies, to my right, thousands of rows of sugarcane and corn. Behind me, a sleeping town, ruled by a hateful, prideful prince; a kingdom of oppression and suffering.

Then I hear a sound. It is not crickets or grasshoppers. It's not the buzzing sound of flying insects. But the sound of a voice. A man's voice. Deep and low. Close.

Frozen on the fence, every fibre of my body vibrating with apprehension, I strain my eyes to see in the lowlight cast by the white moon shining high above the heavens. All I can make out in the faintness is the shape of tall rows of crops.

The voice comes again, closer now. It is a whispering, dull sound, but in the stillness of the night, it may as well be a thundering scream.

Holding my breath as I move gradually and deliberately, as not to make a sound, I lift my left leg over the boundary, and slip down the side of the fence. Landing silently on the sandy ground below, I edge along the edge of the farmlands, my back grazing the rusty bars as I take slow steps.

The crops smell of manure and wet dirt. It's not a pleasing odour, but it is an improvement on the prison cell, where I had to choose a corner in which to do my business.

"Hey!" a voice to my right shouts.

Shit.

I break into a sprint, disappearing into a line of giant sugarcane, praying that the direction I'm heading is south. Hearing heavy footsteps behind me, I am becoming increasingly aware of the fact that I cannot stop running, no matter how my feet ache, or how the brisk air scorches my chest.

I do not know how long I run through the rows of crops, or when my prowlers lose track of me, but after what feels like forever, the row of sugarcanes end, and the iron fence finally comes into view. By light of the moon, I collapse at the edge of the cropland, holding the railing that contains the agriculture in both hands, as I catch my breath.

A dizziness floods my mind and blurs my vision. Vertigo weakens my senses. The sky is the ground, and the ground is the sky, and then they swirl together in a kaleidoscope of darkness. Which way is up, it's like I've never known.

And then I sleep.

Chapter 24

I wake with the sun. I watch as the sky turns from purple to pink to orange, all in a matter of minutes, as the sun begins its daily journey from east to west. To the east, I see now in the daylight a body of water. To the west, more agricultural land, trapped by more iron fence.

I am to continue south, where I now see three colossal mountains looming over the enormous forestry, which spans for countless acres. The sight of the thick trees reminds me of home. Already, I can hear birdsong, melodious shrills resonating through the trees.

At first, it feels peaceful and calm, but then my mind wanders back to my conversations with Pénquil in the prison; the voracious animals that reside in these forests. Wolves. Animals of prey. I find myself hoping that these creatures are well-fed.

All at once, my stomach clenches with hunger. I feel a queasiness churn inside me, a dull pain of starvation in my stomach. How long has it been since I have eaten? It's impossible to know, but by the pit deep in my belly, I imagine that it has been at least a couple of days.

I nick ears of corn from the plants around me, shoving as many into my dress as I can fit. As I tear the green husk, taking my first bite of fresh vegetation in what feels like years, gratitude overwhelms me. I thank the God of Life that there is food available to me, even if I must steal it.

Jumping the fence for a second time, careful to not to drop

the many husks of corn I have thieved from the farm, I head towards the clear blue lake. I have no means of carrying the water with me; not a bottle or a bucket to hold it. So, I decide I must drink as much as I can stomach, as I have no way of knowing whether there will be clean water in the forest through which I will trek to reach the mountains.

Kneeling at the bank of the large pond, I scoop up a handful of cool water and bring it to my dry lips. The water is heavenly. It saturates my thirsty mouth, soothes my parched throat.

Then, only ten or so paces from me, there is the sound of a single splash. It's not great and it's not strident. It is simply a slight *splosh* in the clear water. Seemingly insignificant. The water is so clean and clear that it seems so unlikely that there would be anything large living in it. But perhaps there are fish in the lake. Frogs, maybe.

After I drink, I use the water to wash my face and arms. I rinse my braided hair in the clean water. The freshness of the lake is cold against my sweltering scalp. Daisies from the meadow that had stuck into my hair now fall into the lake at my knees, floating atop the water. I feel the water drip down my face and neck, as I wash my hair, soaking into my black gown.

I should really do something about this dress.

It's so impractical to wear an evening gown on such a perilous adventure through unknown timberlands. It makes running nearly impossible.

Another splash. Closer now.

This time, the sound causes me to pause. Looking out at the clear, still water, I watch, waiting for another sound. I wait to hear or see something move in the depths of the lake.

Then, something does.

A hand, grey and slimy, with yellow claws as long as an

eagle's talon, reaches from the water. It grips my knee with such force that I am pulled under the water. The water is icy, like a pond in the arctic. It impales my skin, solidifies my bones, and makes my body tremor.

Opening my eyes under the water, I see the shadowy shape of a navy-blue fish with arms and a face that appears elven. The skin of the creature is steely-grey with spots of blue speckled haphazardly all over. Black hair surrounds the creature's head, moving independently as though controlled by snakes or worms. It reaches for me again.

I scream.

My screams of horror come out as silent bubbles, rising to the surface of the water and popping high above me. I kick out with both feet. I use all my might to stomp at the outlandish creature.

The monster's grip on my ankle sends shooting pains into my shin, where yellow talons pierce the skin. More shrieking and kicking out at the creature seem to deter it. It shrinks back from me, dropping my ankle, its flippered tail curling around like a seahorse's. Now out of kicking-distance, the beady black eyes drill into me.

A single shrill scream from the sea monster, then the siren, with one dive, plunges deeper into the lake and out of sight. As quickly as it appeared, it is gone.

As I swim away, back to the surface, I can barely believe what I have seen. I've heard stories of them, but none ever seemed plausible – they are a myth! And yet…

Sitting on the bank, now drenched from head to toe, I pick up the ears of corn that I had dropped when I was pulled into the water.

My black ball gown is ruined. There are many rips and tears

in the skirt of the tattered dress, holes here and there that reveal my chocolate brown skin.

Perhaps I was hallucinating. Perhaps starvation has driven me to madness. Perhaps the siren I have seen is some insane delusion, brought about by the famishment and trauma of the last few days.

Or perhaps the myths are true, and sirens truly lurk in cold waters, waiting on a lonely soul, whom they can drag into their depths.

I'm reminded of the stories my father used to tell of sirens taking weary sailors. He never believed them, but I think he relished in the look of shock that coated my face when he described the monsters hauling sailors over the railing of a ship and into the bitter waters of the Havvren Sea.

"And he was pulled overboard by a fearsome creature with the top-half of an elf and the tail of a fish!" my father crowed engagingly. "He floundered frantically in the water, his cries piercing as the monstress pulled him down into the murky depths of the ocean waters!"

"You've seen them?" I was balanced upon his lap, the tender age of six, mesmerised by his enthralling narratives of venture and wonder.

"No!" He laughed, amused at me for believing him.

"Then how do you know it's true?"

"It is just a story," he had told me comfortingly. "Sailors who fall overboard, they love to fabricate tales that make them appear brave and strong."

"So, they lie?"

"Some men lie, Aruniar. That is the truth of it. It is your job to know when a man is lying to you, but never your duty to tell his truths."

"Why would men lie?" I asked him.

"Men lie for many reasons. Some lie for power. Some love. And some, will lie for money or riches," King Kelriaq explained. "But this man, your father, would never lie to you." He placed a light kiss on my forehead, as fathers often do with their young daughters in Nashwalte. "Now, it's time for bed!"

My father tucked me into bed, and I asked him, "But, Father, what if they are real?"

"They aren't, Aruniar. They never were."

Holding the hem of the torn black skirt in my fist, I tear the bottom of the dress, attempting to guide the rip straight across, so that I am merely shortening the length of the gown. It makes a dreadful shredding sound, as though I were trying to force myself into a garment that is many sizes too small.

Looking at the dress, now even more ragged than before, the hem a tattered line of jagged fabric that reaches as far as my knee in some places, I feel guilt strike my heart.

Pénquil made this dress. She altered it specifically for me; my taste, my style, my measurements. And now it is ruined.

I allow myself a moment to grieve the dress, before I leave the torn pieces of fabric beside the lake, and start south. I leave the farmlands and treacherous lake behind me, as I enter the forest, armed only with four ears of corn, and ruined ball gown.

Even by the day, the forest is dark. The black silhouettes of murky tree trunks and branches block out any sunshine that might hope to pierce the heavy canopy. The ground beneath my bare feet is damp, thick with leaf litter and mossy forest floor. It's a little slippery with slime as I take careful and deliberate steps through the woods.

It is noiseless. Every so often, I hear the occasional bird song in the distance, and then the trees return to ear-splitting silence.

In the damp of the forest, the humidity sticks to me. It feels clammy and stifling, so that I am reminded of the tropical jungles back home. The way the cool wind carries strident birdsong and the rustle of noisy branches and leaves. The way the gusts howl and cry as they whistle between trees, striking nervousness of uncertainty into my heart.

As I walk further into the silent forest, I now notice that the trees have dark, moist trunks that are wider in circumference than I am tall. Moss and funguses grow both on the surrounding trees, and the forest floor, the leaf litter and fine dirt. In some parts, the ground is wet, causing my toes to sink beneath the surface, mud squelching between my toes.

My mind wanders to Frewope the Devoted, her jungle in Nashwalte. I can't feel her here, in this forest, as I can in the jungle back home. Back home, the jungle practically moves with life, sounds from every direction. How is it that a forest as green as this is so empty?

I imagine that if Frewope the Devoted were here in this forest, her heart would break for the silence that resides here, for the animals that do not live in these trees.

I do not know how long I walk for before the dark forest grows ever darker. As the sun dips lower in the sky, disappearing behind the horizon, I feel the heat of the forest begin to vanish. The cool air nips at my arms, and I wrap them around myself.

The journey is more challenging in the darkness. Now that I cannot make out the driest parts to walk on, my bare feet slip clumsily on the slick forest floor. At one point, in the murky moisture of the damp forest floor, I fall, face-first, into the leaf litter at my feet.

"God of Death, spare me this agony," I mutter bitterly, holding my weight on my hands as I stare down at the wet dirt beneath me.

That's when I hear a rustle in a bush only a few paces of my left, and Pénquil's words come rushing back to me, ringing in my ears, as an unexpected warning: *You must make sure that you build a fire before dark, so that you can see the wolves coming at night.*

Shit.

In the darkness, I make out a shape. Terror causes my heart to stop as the dark figure moves in my direction. I have no choice.

I run.

Never mind the dirt and leaves that stick stubbornly to my skin; I am sprinting now, through the forest. My feet slide on leaves and moss. I take huge strides. I hear my blood pulsing in my ears. My heart thrums in my chest.

At some point, I lose my ears of corn, dropping them haphazardly somewhere deep in the woods. Although it is a loss, I tell myself that I will find more food when the sun comes up.

When I am sure that I have outrun whatever creature I saw in the shadows back there, I return to a walking pace, my heart pounding and my breath coming in deep wheezes. I cough, the only sound in this noiseless place, and decide it is time to stop for the night.

I'll have to build a fire.

It takes some time to gather enough wood from the fallen branches and sticks upon the forest floor – Frewope the Devoted would be most angry if she witnessed the Princess of Nashwalte breaking branches of trees to make a fire! When I have enough, I sit on the leaf litter and start a small fire with two sticks, as I have seen cooks back home do with the outdoor oven.

The trees around me glow in the dimness, the orange flame

casting light across the small patch of forest that looms around me. The heat of the fire is welcome, soothing my skin and healing the rise of goose bumps.

High above me, in the canopy, I hear the occasional crunch of leaves and whining of branches under a creature's weight. I assume the birds are roosting for the night, taking shelter in trees around me.

I prey to the Goddess Frewope that it not something larger.

I no longer shiver, and sleep creeps up on me the way I imagine the God of Death might creep up on an elderly king. As I curl into a ball at the edge of the fire, my eyes slip closed, and tiredness overcomes me. I drift into a peaceful dream of home, and I no longer feel afraid.

***

I wake to the sound of birdsong and continue my journey. With uncertainty of the way to the mountains from here, I simply continue south, using the rising sun as a guide.

The forest is warm during the day and sweat beads at my forehead and top lip.

Stopping at ponds and streams of running water, I drink from my cupped hands, and rinse my hair to cool down. The water feels cold and soothing on my hot skin. I use the water to clean cuts on my legs from sticks and branches. This time, I am wary of sea creatures that may pull me in to drown.

Since I have lost my corn, I eat the strange pink and yellow fruits called unicorn apples as I continue my journey. I also notice tiny red berries and strange pods that hang from thin trees – but Hazel trained me well.

"Never eat things that you are not sure of!" she would tell

me strictly. "Any fruit or nut could be lethal, if you do not know its origin!"

It's about midday when the sun is high above me in the blue sky, beating down, burning the back of my neck and shoulders, my skin hot to the touch. My feet ache, swollen and blistered from loose gravel and rocky terrain. Sweat rolls down the sides of my face, collecting in puddles on my chest and the back of my neck.

When I notice a sudden incline of terrain, I prey to the God of Life that I have finally found the mountain upon which there is a hidden village, and that Pénquil will be there, waiting for me.

I let the image of her, with her long, golden hair and her shimmering emerald eyes, engulf my attention, as I climb the steep mountain, clutching clumps of grass and large rocks for stability.

As the forest falls away with the increase in altitude, I feel the temperature begin to drop. I shiver with the cool wind that rattles through me.

Finally, as pink and orange stream across the sky, I reach the peak of the mountain. From here, I can see the canopy of forest that surround. I see two more mountains to the south, and the ocean to the east. Far away, in the west, I see the glow of Whŷstelkịné. Beyond the town, I see the castle in the far-off distance, where my father lays dead in the West Wing, and my heart squeezes.

As I turn on the spot, looking all around me, taking in the spectacular view, one thing is abundantly clear; Pénquil is not here.

Grey smoke rises south-east of me, maybe halfway down the mountain, and hope that perhaps Pénquil will be there flutters eagerly in my chest.

Chapter 25

By the time I reach the source of the smoke, the sky is hazy, and the sun has set, leaving the thickening forest around me in complete darkness. The air, now halfway down the mountain side, is not quite as cold as it had been at the peak – but it still holds goose bumps on my exposed arms and shoulders, a prickle of a shiver on my neck.

A smell lingers in the air. Food. It smells like meat. It reminds me of the pan-fried meats back home in Willcrest; the herbs and spices that entirely covered the taste of the meat, so that whatever you were eating was totally unrecognisable. Fish, chicken, venison, pork – with the amount of seasoning Nashwaltians use, it's all identical.

Although the fire has died down, there is still a dim, orange glow from the smouldering logs. No sign of others, apart from a single footstep in the loose sand.

Disappointment rings in my chest. I had hoped to find Pénquil sitting by the fire, her gown ripped like mine, that long, blonde hair tied back from a dirty, freckled face. That smile that I've come to love – I long for it. I long to see it.

Slow and careful steps lead me to a spot on the green grass beside the fire. It's warm here. With the warmth from the flames, and the same of freshly cooked food, beside this fire is the safest I have felt in days.

The smell of the burnt flavouring, mixed with the distinctive scent of meat, has my stomach twisting and snarling with hunger.

I feel my tongue salivating, desperate for a taste of it.

Will anyone be coming back for it? Would they mind if I had a taste?

I can't imagine any stranger being thrilled to coming back to their camp to find their food has been stolen. The guilt that ticks inside me is the only thing that stops me from snatching the meat from the fire and eating it.

Instead, I wait. I wait to see if anyone will come back to eat the meal that they have cooked on the open flames.

While I wait, I massage my aching feet. There are large, round blisters forming on the soles of my feet, cuts and scratches along my soft skin. My feet have never been bare, they have never trekked this far, especially without shoes.

I wait for what feels like an eternity. Desperately, I watch the meat blacken with burnt edges, sizzling and crunching over the heat of the fire.

The smell makes my mouth water. It causes an involuntary gurgling in my empty stomach.

Finally, I give in. I stab the meat out of the fire with a nearby stick, and let it cool in the cold night air before I finally bite into it. The juices and oil from the meat run down my hands to my elbows, slip down my chin and drip onto my tattered dress. I am sure that if anyone caught me now, sitting beside a fire, eating like a banshee, they would believe I am a beast of the forest, an animalistic creature, desperate for the taste of blood.

It is not like a princess. It is not charming. It is not attractive.

When I have eaten the meat I've stolen from the blaze, I wipe my mouth and hands on my dress – it's ruined anyway. Then, I curl up into a ball on the grass alongside the flames, using my elbow as a pillow under my head.

The sounds of the forest comfort me. Birds calling, trees

rustling, the wind howling through the branches, crickets chirping to each other in the long grass.

Although Pénquil may not be here, it comforts me to know that there is the possibility that she has been.

After some time of laying on the grass, trying to sleep, the sound of footsteps stirs me. I do not move, but simply open one eye to survey.

Figures, like shadows, pace along the trees. People.

Briefly, I wonder whether they could be Prince Fravine's men, looking for me. Hunting me, like a tiger hunts the elk.

They speak in hushed voices; in a language I don't understand. At first, they are skittish, watching me from the trees, talking quietly, as though they are afraid to wake me. I give no sign that I am awake; I keep as still as possible, watching only with one eye open.

Then, they surround me. At only a pace away, I am completely still, waiting for what will happen next.

One grabs my arm.

Another has me by the foot.

A third holds a spear at me.

My heart races. The pounding in my ears makes it impossible to hear anything else.

I scream, as they lift me from the ground, kicking out at them. I feel my heart pounding in my throat and my chest. A coldness aches in my legs. My stomach lurches with sickness.

"Release me!" I shout at them.

They do not reply.

Dryness seizes my mouth, dizziness swirls my vision. My breath catches in my chest, burning my lungs and I cannot breathe. I hurt my wrist trying to punch the one who holds me by the hands; my ankles twist painfully in the palm of the person who holds me by my legs. No matter which way I try to turn, no matter the amount of force I put into my kicks and punches, these strangers are stronger than me.

My efforts are useless as I struggle against them.

They speak in a language I don't know, but not to me; they are speaking to each other. They pay me no mind, as they carry me over their shoulders, as though I weigh nothing.

All the ease and contentment I had felt by the fire has long dissolved now. The hope of finding Pénquil has vanished.

I feel helpless.

I feel alone.

Chapter 26

As one might expect from a group of strange people living in the forest, who have strung up their hostage like an offering to the Gods, they take me to their leader. They carry me through the forest. As more and more people appear, I start to wonder whether this is the village that Pénquil told me about.

A chanting starts, as the two that hold me in their hands, one at my arms and one at my feet, lift me ever higher into the air. Now, I hang over their heads, totally at their mercy. They shake me up and down, and I feel the sickness from earlier well in the pit of my stomach.

Then, I am dropped.

I feel the air whoosh past my hair and skirt, as I land heavily on the grass. It knocks the wind out of me. A sound escapes me. A sort of grunt, mixed with a high-pitched whimper. My side aches and I wonder whether I have broken a rib.

A loud voice speaks in a language I don't understand.

When I finally will myself to look up, I see someone very tall, wearing a dress made of leaves and flowers, standing over me. Their black ringlets hang at either side of their head, and they're looking at me as though I am a cockroach that has wandered into their midst, uninvited.

A branch, knobbed and rough, pokes under my chin. A firmness behind it forces me to raise my head off the grass, though, it hurts to do so – everything hurts.

"I am Jŏriia, Queen of the Dãįpsŷr." Her pronunciation is

thick, barely understandable, but I recognise that her drawl sounds like Pénquil's. Like a Whŷstelkịnér. "We have resided in this forest for generations. Never have I seen an elf quite like you."

I do not speak as the queen looks me up and down, her grey eyes penetrating and criticising. It reminds me a little too much of Queen Nyssra.

"Your name?" the Queen of Dãịpsŷr says.

Carefully, I push my weight onto my hands and pull myself up. When I try to stand, however, the branch, still held at my neck, pushes into my skin. I feel it press firmly against my throat, cutting my breath for a second.

"Princess Aruniar of Nashwalte," I manage.

"What are you doing here?"

"I... I ran from Prince Frąviné. He was going to kill me—"

"No," Queen Jŏriia cuts me off. "I mean, what are you doing here? On this island. Nashwalte is, no doubt, far from here, is it not?"

"Nashwalte is six days travel across the Havvren Sea."

"So, what are you doing here?"

I take a breath, moving an inch away from the branch that scratches against my throat, but it follows me, against my neck again.

"I came to marry the prince."

"Prince Frąviné?"

"Yes."

"And now he is going to kill you?" She doesn't sound surprised; just interested. Her grey eyes pour into me, watching me so closely that I begin to wonder if she was an eagle in another life.

"Pénquil said it would be safe here."

There's a soft murmur that drifts through the crowd that

surrounds us – I had nearly forgotten that they were there.

"Pénquil…" Queen Jŭriia says her name so thoughtfully that it makes a flutter of hope spark in my stomach, forces a tiny smile onto my lips.

"Is she here?"

"Pénquil is my child," the queen tells me. Her voice is tender as she adds, "I rescued her when she was very young. I have not seen her in many months."

"What did you rescue her from?"

"Royalty."

My mind buzzes with questions, with wonderings.

"Pénquil is not here?" I clarify.

The queen frees my neck from the branch in her hand. She steps back from me, releasing a heavy breath as she uses the stick in her hand to hold her weight. Her greyish eyes are sympathetic as she looks back at me.

"My daughter has not been here almost a year." She says it so miserably that I feel a twinge of gloom for her. A mother who has not seen their child in a long time. "But she will be back. When the time comes, we will see her again."

Disappointment swarms my heart. I had hoped that Pénquil was here, hiding in the trees.

"No, Your Grace—"

"Jŭriia is fine," she corrects me, her voice smooth and calm as she speaks, like the salty wind over the sea.

"Jŭriia," I restart. "Pénquil is in danger."

Although the people around us start to chatter, confused mumbles rippling through the surrounding area, the queen watches me for a moment, her eyes serious. She says nothing, waiting for me to continue.

"The prince was going to kill us both. He locked us up in the dungeons below the city," I explain. My breath catches in my throat as I remember it, my mouth going dry.

"Where is she now?" The queen does not appear worried, just curious.

"I don't know," I tell her honestly. "She ran off into the forest. She left me."

It's silent around me. No one speaks now. I find myself wondering whether it is fear or curiosity that stifles the villager's whisperings.

The queen's grey eyes watch me in a way that reminds me startlingly of Pénquil.

"She will be fine," the queen decides. "My daughter has grown up in these forests. In these mountains, she is home."

I'm about to protest, but she holds up a hand to stop me. "You are welcome to stay as long as you need. Any friend of Pénquil is a friend of Dãipsŷr."

And with that, she is gone. Her gown of flowers and leaves swishes noiselessly as she turns from me, sweeping back towards a small building, made from twigs and branches, leaned against the trunk of a thick maple tree.

Around me, the crowd disperses. I watch as several people climb up trees and disappear among the branches. Others walk into the darkness of the forest. And I am left alone.

Again.

Late that night, when the sun has set and the woods are quiet, Dãipsŷr villagers gather in small groups, sitting cross-legged on the sandy ground of the forest, a fire crackling at the centre of the group. Some hold pieces of charred meat in their hands, others lie on their backs, their stomachs full of the evening meal.

Children sit in the laps of their parents. Couples wrap arms around each other. Friends talk in loud voices, laughing and sharing stories.

Alone at the edge of the gathering, I sit curled up against at tree, legs curled up against my chest. The smell of food causes my stomach to groan and ache with hunger.

After some time of darkness, long after night has fallen, I see four young men stand and head to the fire in the middle of the gathering place. I watch them squash green leaves in their hands, the forest rumbling with murmured voices. The four men speak in murmured voices, then blow the crushed-up leaves into the fire, through cupped hands over their mouths.

The flames seem to grow wider and taller as the blaze engulfs the leaves. A menacing crackling from deep within the flames startles me. Unnatural green smoke rises from the smouldering logs. With the smoke comes a familiar smell that I can't quite place.

Her gown of flowers dragging along the leaf litter behind her, Queen Jŭriia strides alongside the fire. The green glow of the flames reflects acutely on her light skin as she regards the villagers that surround her. Then she turns, spinning theatrically on the ball of her foot to face the flames, her shawl of flowers flaring dramatically around her.

"Gods of the Forest!" she announces, voice echoing through the trees. "I call upon you. Please come out, so that we may talk!"

The forest is silent. The ominous flames do not change.

I find myself looking around. Perhaps I hope that the Forest Gods will show themselves.

"Gods of the Forest, I must speak with you!" Queen Jŭriia shouts, now raising her arms to the green flames. "Show yourselves!"

The villagers that surround do not make a sound. Everyone is utterly silent as the queen calls to the gods again, this time her tone frantic. Desperate. There's almost a tinge of fear in her voice that I would only associate with the love of a terrified mother.

Still, the forest is silent.

"It is important!" she screams at the flames.

I see the hope fading in the queen's face as her head hangs towards the ground. Her shoulders slump and she lets out a defeated sigh.

The village is hushed with despair as the queen stands at the green blaze, flames dancing threateningly and black smoke rising through the dark canopy.

Either out of disappointment, or out of respect for the required privacy of their heartbroken queen, the village disperses. As people climb up the trees and disappear among the leafy branches, the fire returns to the ordinary orange glow.

When everyone is gone, I hear the queen whisper through thick tears, "Please, just bring my daughter back to me."

Chapter 27

It is days before I hear another thing about Pénquil. For nearly a week, I sit by the tree that I have chosen as my own, curled up in a ball at the trunk. I listen to birds chirp, I watch the branches of the thick forest sway in the breeze. People pass me, but no one speaks to me. Sometimes, people offer me food or water. Most times, I turn them down.

On the fifth day of waiting, I hear an unfamiliar sound; cheering. Excited voices, whooping and shouts, carried through the canopies of the forest.

What could that be?

And then I see it. A crowd of people, walking together as one. They group together in a way that suggests they are all carrying a single item. They're singing. Joyous. Celebrating.

From the safety of my tree, I watch expectantly as the crowd grows closer and closer. I strain my ears to listen – it is no use, the only person to speak a common language is the queen, and I haven't seen her since my arrival.

Then I see her.

Blonde hair, shimmering in the sunlight. Pointed ears that poke out of her hair. A red dress, velvet and warm in the light of the morning.

Pénquil. It's her.

My strides are quick and long as I sprint across the tall grass, closing the space between us. Never mind my bruised and blistered feet. Pay no mind to the ache in my side from where I was dropped on the grass. Nothing matters, except for…

As I stand in front of her, it's as though the world moves in slow motion. I stare at her freckled face, trying to hold onto this moment, to capture it, in case I ever lose her again. She hasn't noticed me yet; she is laughing with the villagers, speaking a language I do not know.

Despite the smile on her features, she looks dishevelled.

There is mud in her gold hair, a deep cut along her chest; her velvet dress is torn in several places, revealing purple bruising on her back and shoulders. And yet, she is still the most beautiful sight to behold.

Then, Pénquil's eyes, green as emeralds, catch mine. She and I look at each other, over the shoulder of a villager who can't be more than twelve years of age. For the first time in days, I feel safe.

"Aruniar?" My name on her lips makes my whole body shake. "Is that you?"

I watch her green eyes as they gaze into mine, and I feel my heartbeat about a million times a minute.

I can't breathe.

I can't speak.

I try to talk, but no sound comes out. When all else fails, I shove villagers aside; I take her in my arms; I hold her firm against me, her back warm on my hands; and my lips finally touch hers. Her lavender smell is warm and welcome in my nose. I soak it up, breathing deeply as we kiss, my arms so tight around her that I am nearly worried about breaking a rib. Her sweet taste fills my mouth, a taste so familiar that, even though my home is a hundred miles away, I am sure that I have found it.

After what feels like the longest time, we are together again, and – even though my father is dead, Hazel is gone, there is no way to go back to Nashwalte, and we have been sentenced to death by the person I was supposed to marry – all is right in the world.

Because we are together.

Chapter 28

A little while later, we are seated around a fire, several villagers sitting with us, sharing meat they've cooked and vegetables they've foraged. The food is delicious, and it smells like seasoning. It smells like the meats cooked back home.

When Pénquil and I are sitting together with a handful of food each, and all the other villagers are busy with their own conversations, she tells me about her travels from Whŷstelkiné.

"Why did it take you so long?" I ask her. "I thought you were gone. Or dead. I was so worried."

"On the first night, I slept on the north side of the forest, near a lake," Pénquil explains. "I waited for you there, and I thought I would be safe from the wolves, if I built a fire. I thought I would be able to wait for you, and you'd come with me."

"What happened?"

"Well, I woke up in the middle of the night, and there was howling." Pénquil's voice is quiet. She's whispering, as though she thinks that there are wolves nearby that might overhear us. "I thought if I was quiet, they wouldn't come near me. I don't know what I was thinking. It was stupid."

"Did they attack you?"

"Four of them," Pénquil nods. She takes a bite from the meat in her hand, which I now know was once a small bird. "Massive, too. They stalked me for a while, hiding in the forest. I knew they were there."

"Didn't you run?"

"Not at first. I was so weak from being locked up in the dungeon. I was starved. I didn't have the energy to run."

"What did you do?"

"They attacked me. One got me here." She points to the open wound on her chest, a claw mark from a paw the size of my hand. "It bled for a few days."

I can't imagine the size of the creature that would have done that. To have paws that size... it must nearly be the size of a horse! Do wolves even grow that big?

Pénquil continues, "Another one bit me."

She moves to gesture to her knee, where there are two gaping holes in her joint. I lean forward, looking closely at her wound. It is deep, and desperately needs to be cleaned; there is dried blood all around it yellow pus weeping from it. Already, it is becoming infected. The sight of it makes my stomach curl with uneasiness.

"Here," I tell her gently, reaching out to touch her knee.

Although Hazel had been my maid for many years, she didn't teach me much about Old Medicine. She only showed me a couple of healing potions. One is good for cuts and open wounds like these; it will ward off infection, at the very least.

Pénquil flinches back from me, horror in her eyes. I see her chest quivering and my stomach twists with guilt. I never wanted to make her afraid of me.

"Let me help. I can make some medicine." I use a soft voice to speak to her, trying to be as gentle as possible.

Finally, even with fear in her eyes, she relents, allowing me to touch her knee. After a quick inspection, I take a small daisy from the grass beneath us and crush it in my fist. Licking my fingers and rubbing the saliva between my thumb and forefinger, I use several daisies to make a paste.

"Frewope, devoted god, please lend me your power," I whisper to the flowers as I crush them between my fingers.

Just as I finish the incantation, the flowers begin to glow.

Pénquil is staring at me, her eyes wide. At first, I can't tell if it's fear or disgust I see in her expression. She doesn't move, completely frozen as she watches me smear the crushed-up daisies over her wound.

"I know it looks disgusting," I tell her with a self-conscious laugh. "But don't worry. It will help."

Pénquil doesn't look convinced, so I change the subject. "How did you get away?"

"Guess I was lucky" is all Pénquil offers as an explanation.

She stares into the dark forest, her gaze entirely absent. She looks tired. Defeated, exhausted. She is beautiful, no doubt about it, but something about her appears much older than she had in the tunnel. Withered.

It's quiet between us for a few minutes, the only sound the crackling of the fire.

"So, Queen Jŭriia says you're her daughter," I say.

There's a question there. I've been thinking about it for days, that weird exchange. How Queen Jŭriia had said that she saved Pénquil from royalty.

A thought had occurred to me – but it's absurd! It's just a story.

Pénquil's eyes linger on the darkness for a little while longer, glazed over with dullness. Her mouth is a straight line. I begin to wonder whether she had heard me. And then she takes a deep breath.

"Queen Jŭriia, my tidda, rescued me from Whŷstelkiné when I was a baby," she whispers. Her voice is so quiet, I must strain my ears to hear her at all.

"What do you mean 'rescued'?" I clarify.

Again, I start to wonder whether she's heard me; she doesn't speak for a while. She doesn't look at me either. She's starting straight ahead, eyes unmoving. Her emerald eyes flicker in the light of the fire.

I'm about to repeat myself when she says, "She stole me."

"From…?"

Finally, her eyes meet mine. Her face is unreadable. Her expression is closed. As she looks at me, nothing changes on her face. Her gaze is piercing. It's intruding. It's so strong that I have to stop myself from looking away.

There is such hesitation in the way that she waits, that I know what she is about to say.

"From the royals," Pénquil finally answers.

I feel like I should be surprised. I think that I should be outraged. I don't know what an expected reaction should be to this information – but I don't feel anything. Maybe I knew all along.

"Why did she take you?" I manage.

Pénquil releases a long and slow sigh, finally turning away from me, and back towards the fire.

"I think it was to teach the king and queen a lesson. I think it was to prevent more suffering," Pénquil explains. Her voice is a little hoarse, a bit gruff in the cool of the night. "But they made more heirs, of course. They moved on. No one even mentions Princess Lãswei anymore. Most people in Whŷstelkiné don't even know who she is."

"She is you."

"Aruniar, she is the Princess of Whŷstelkiné. I am Pénquil, the merchant."

"You could be the Princess of Whŷstelkiné."

"I couldn't." Pénquil shakes her head. "No one would believe that I am a princess. Not even Queen Nyssra herself would recognise me now."

"We could try."

"They will never listen."

"Then we could form an army!" I argue, suddenly hit with a burst of revengeful energy. "We will fight against the royal family, and we will conquer them!"

A chuckle wriggles its way through Pénquil's body. She looks at me with such affection that I'm sure I will combust at the mere expression on her face.

"With what army?" She chuckles.

"Look around," I tell her. "There must be at least two hundred people in this village, right? Surely, they will fight for you, the daughter of their queen?"

Consideration flickers across Pénquil's face for a moment. For a few seconds, I think that I have convinced her. For a minute, I believe that I am about to start a war with the Prince of Whŷstelkiné. And then, with a small shake of Pénquil's head, it's gone.

"These people will not fight," she decides.

She uses her hands to lift herself off the grass and stands before me. Looking down at me with a soft smile, she holds out a hand to help me up.

"How do you know?" I press.

"Aruniar, please," she sighs. "I don't want to argue."

"I am not arguing!"

"I am very tired. I had a very long journey." She does sound exhausted. Her voice is soft and winded. "Let's just go to bed, please."

But I cannot let it go. "Pénquil, these people love you! You are their princess."

"They came here for peace."

"You can give them peace, in Whŷstelkịné!"

Pénquil's sigh is heavy. She is tired. Her eyes close as she runs a hand through her hair, her long fingers combing through the roots. She is so beautiful in the moonlight that bounces off her face that I don't know how I ever could have lived without her.

"We will lose," she tells me in a whisper. "Queen Nyssra has an army of a thousand men. To fight them would be in vain. It is pointless."

Finally, I accept that perhaps Pénquil is right.

We climb to the top of a large tree in the village, where I, for the first time in my life, fall asleep beside a woman. Together, this night, and every night after, we sleep in each other's arms, nestled together under the green canopy of the forest. Safe, in a new home.